The Haunted Life Of Violet

Talia Atkins

CONTENTS

A message from the author.

There is a full list of TW on the last page. Please take the time to read them through before proceeding. There is a list of TW that is permanently pinned on my instagram page. It includes my previously released books as well.

My cult books are raw and unfiltered. They are dark and tabo0 and should only be read if you are over the age of 18.

Thank you to everyone that keeps showing up for me, and showing my books so much love.

To the ones that were waiting for someone to be your saviour.

Sometimes you have to become your own saviour.

TWENTY YEARS AGO

S ome would say they were scared of the dark. Some would say they would stay clear of the lingering shadows because they don't know what horrors could be hidden in them. For me? I fantasize over being in the cold clutches of ink. Being blind in pitch black nothingness seems like a fate I would never experience. Instead, I am not blind. I am not deaf and I feel too much.

Women shouldn't feel, they shouldn't speak and they should never observe anything that may or may not be happening around them. We just simply *are*. Here, yet not here. Not to be seen or heard. The lashings we would receive if we spoke would soon remind us that we do not have any rights to have a voice.

My soft white dress presses gently against my knees as I lean over our small table and clear away Father's cutlery. I look around our small cabin, the constant earthy smell reminding me that soon summer will be upon us and the moss won't be as bad. It will be warmer.

"Warmer..." I whisper as quietly as possible. I slam my lips together while I place the kitchenware into our small basin and run some water over them. My hair hangs loosely around my face, like a curtain protecting me from any spirits that may have heard me speaking out of turn. My back could be scarred from that moment of weakness. I place the cutlery on the bench to drip dry, knowing I am late for my next lot of chores. I have to sweep the large community hall out so that it's completely clear of leaves and dirt.

All the adults were led deep into the forest where cleansing ceremonies are held, but not us children though. We do jobs while the male children watch our every move. If we go against the way of our village, they would tell the leading father, and he would then hand out our punishment.

As I walk across the grassy area toward the large community hall, I hear a ruckus. Screams and then loud bangs that scared the birds from our trees. I frown and look up toward the sky where the birds frantically try and fly away as far as they can. That doesn't normally happen with ceremonies. Normally the crows go toward the ceremony.

As my bare feet touch the rugged timber that is the bottom step, I hear Dad yelling. His voice is urgent, but I don't want to look back. I'm not allowed to show any hint that I am thinking of my own accord. What if it is a test? I can't have any sort of response unless I am spoken to directly.

I wish I could be like the other women here who see nothing and notice nothing. I wish the only thing I want in my life is to please the brothers and fathers in our village like them. The gods blessed them. The brothers and fathers know how to keep our race pure, to make sure when we die, we go to the sky gods that will look after our souls.

But I'm not like them; I notice everything around me. Even when my eyes are low and directed at the ground, I seem to take in everything around me. I whisper words I shouldn't but I like how they feel on my tongue. I like the sound of my own voice. It's light. Musical. I think the devils have touched my essence and I am not for the sky gods. I trace my bottom lip with my tongue and walk up the last step, ignoring the thought that begs for my attention. Crows do gods' work. They are the gate keepers and they haven't come for me. They don't feast on my flesh, yet.

"Violet!" My blood father's voice grates over my ears. His voice has never been a kind one. I turn to him now that my name has been spoken. I chomp down on the inside of my cheek as I punish myself for having an opinion on how his voice has been toward me.

I pivot on the step while keeping my shoulders hunched and head hung low. I'm thankful for my long sandy colored hair, because it feels like a protective shield to some of the emotional waves that I want to shy away from. It feels unnatural for me to stand so still and take anything and everything the brothers and fathers want to unleash on us.

His rugged, overworked hands wrap around my immature shoulders and squeeze tightly. I catch sight of the dirt under his nails as they leave small crescent-shaped brown marks on my white gown. His hot breath rushes against my solemn face as he speaks in a rush. "We are leaving.

Your mother has a backpack she is retrieving. Then we will be on our way." His voice is frantic. *Scared.*

I want to ask him where we are going. The question burns in me, intensifying with every passing moment. But as Mom rushes over with the backpack and hands it off to Dad, he purposely slashes a sharp hunting knife up into her rib cage. I can see it play out without having to raise my head. If I raise my head, I may be next. Why would he do that? She crumples to the ground and clutches at her torso. Slowly, her eyes become dull as the wheezing stops.

"Your brother is meeting us past the clearing. We are tramping over the mountains, where our father cult group resides."

CHAPTER 1

P resent day

"Fuck," I breathe as my manacle chain gets caught on the loose nail on the timber-laid flooring. I bend down, rubbing my ankle and angrily glare at the copper nail that ruthlessly sticks out. As I try to slip the tip of my finger down the iron clasp around my leg, I break a fingernail off. I land on my ass and punch the floor out of sheer anger.

The round door handle rattles and with a loud slow groan, the door pushes open. Father leader is in the doorway and his eyes creep around the small room before they finally land on me. He glares down at me, and the weight of his displeasured stare makes me wither uncomfortably and hang my head low with my knees folded under my chin.

"You are meant to have the candles all made by now," his deep voice growls at me.

"I-I have finished. I was inspecting the nail sticking out. It catches on my manacles," I assure him quietly.

His heavy footsteps send a subtle shake through the cabin as he nears. He crouches low and flicks the nail with his calloused finger before turning his head to me.

"You have a hammer. Fix it. Where are the candles, Violet?"

I raise my hand slowly and lift a finger, so I am pointing to the shelf on the opposite wall. He grunts then stands and walks to where I directed him.

He lifts one of the small iron candle holders and inspects the fresh wax that now fills it.

"Good," he says, then angles himself toward me again. His eyes are evil. He does evil things. I don't like being in his line of sight.

I like to be hidden in here. My cabin is my solitude. Although the old wood has lost its rich color and it pales now with mossy growth framing it, it is still mine.

"You are to come to the mating ceremony tonight," he orders me. His word is the law.

But I didn't expect that. No one ever wants me at the ceremonies. They like me in here. Hidden, making medicines and candles. The shock leaves me in a moment of weakness and before I can catch myself, I toss my head to the side and meet his gaze head on. He lowers his eyes, with his brows furrowing in the middle, showing me how unhappy he is with my directness.

"I never go to those."

He makes a fist and crunches his knuckles with his other hand, making them crack loudly. I wince and drop my gaze, hanging my head low again.

He won't use his fists to hurt me though. No, he will use his bat with barbed wire wrapped around the end of it or his long thin piece of bamboo. Those are his favorites. He is intimidating me, reminding me I can only speak when I'm being asked a question that requires an answer. I have learnt over the years that some questions do not require an answer and when I dared to question anything, I required a lashing on my behind to jog my memory.

"Do not be late. Sundown. No earlier, no later." His voice rumbles through the stale air and bounces against the walls. Slamming the door loudly, he leaves my small space. A shiver runs through me as I stand and look around for my small hammer.

I stumble over to it, the clinking of iron following me with every step. I grab it and kneel down by the loose nail and hit it as hard as I can. The nail goes in cleanly but I don't feel satisfied so I slam the hammer down again and again. A circular dent appears around the tiny nail and I stop.

The last thing I want to see is one of the sisters being raped by a heap of men.

The antiseptic salve requires my attention today. I pull my stone bowl from under the bench and place it on the rickety timber as I mechanically begin to pour in my base oil and different herbs. I have made jars of this for our doctor countless times. My worn hands catch my attention, causing me to pause for a brief moment. A lone tear runs down my cheek and drops on my dress when I make the mistake of dwelling that I am thirty now. And in thirty years, I will still be staring out of this same cobweb ridden window.

The toxic berries and herbs on the highest shelf draw me in. They have so many times before as I wondered if the black shadows could give me relief and a peaceful silence.

But my bad habit of wanting my heart to beat and my body to feel warm won out every single time.

As I grind the turmeric with my smooth rock, I fantasize over grinding someone's blood and bones with my bare hands. The shadows used to cling to my desperate thoughts, and now they are painted in vibrant red. It's not my own life I want to take with the toxic jars on my shelf, it's theirs. Just once, I would like to be able to let loose and have a way with a bound body and no boundaries in my way. Sadistic thoughts of the males fill my head.

With a loud sigh, I push the concoction away from me and turn my back to it. I rest my hands on the countertop behind me and lean my weight on them, my eyes settling on the black gown hanging off a hook above my cot. It only gets worn at mating ceremonies. They say we wear white to show our purity, but we wear black this one night to act as invisible witnesses in the dead of the night. We are not to be seen; we are not to speak. We need to just stand there in black to make sure it is completed correctly.

I'm lucky I never had a mating ceremony. My brother and I were used as examples of what happens to leftovers from cults that fall apart and don't follow the laws within themselves.

We were destined to live here with no partners and no future children. For this, I am glad, though my brother never took it as well. He is resentful but saves his resentment for me.

I push off the bench and run my fingers through my long brunette hair. I will have to braid my hair before tonight as well. I roll my eyes and turn back to the bench once more. I bash the rock against the future salve and pretend it is the father leader's head. Damn him for not leaving me alone and content in my workspace.

CHAPTER 2

The smell of melting wax is pungent in the soft whispering night breeze. Some of my most haunting memories have the same poignant aromas linked to them. It's sentimental to me in all the wrong ways.

I keep my hands behind my back, fingers loosely linked together with my black satin hood completely covering my face. I keep my head low, letting the sisters' feet in front of me show me the way I need to go. We walk single file into the waiting half circle of men. All forty-seven of us.

We make two rows, very quietly, just the soft sound of flowing fabric swaying and crackling of branches on the fire filling our secluded space. The thick growth of trees completely surrounds us, with nothing but a narrow worn dirt path leading in and out of the ceremonial clearing.

Because of where I entered the gathering line back in the village, it put me in the front row. I cringe and gnaw at my bottom lip as I think about the sight I am about to witness. I have only been to one ceremony when I was a lot younger and there is no part of me that ever wanted to come to another one.

Slowly, we all look up and set our gazes on the girl in front of us. She is so young. I sympathize with her because this was so close to being my life. Had it not been for our village home falling apart, I would have had a ceremony similar to this. But it would have been in a lone cabin, on a concrete slab. A tremor runs through my hands as I allow myself a brief moment to think of my past home. Birdie was the last one to be mated on that slab and after that, we all fell apart. I was happy for her arrival at first, since her sharp tongue made me curious, until they all left me and I spent weeks hiking the mountains to this place that is more hellish in comparison.

The one thing that followed me from that village to this one—is my inability to quiet my mind and become subservient to the ways of the brothers and fathers. Physically, I follow their rules, their laws. Mentally, I am talking back and judging every single one of them.

I shake my head, banishing the unworthy thoughts from my stubborn mind.

Flames crackle and lick at the still night sky. It casts an orange hue over the naked girl in front of us. She stands in front of a wooden frame. It looks like a seat that has been pushed over. But the leather loops on it make it the mating frame. Orange shimmers over her bare nipples as they harden under the rising moon. She really is beautiful, even if she is only sixteen.

Her hair is much darker than mine and is braided down to the delicate curve above her hips. When she is mated, she will be welcomed to cut some of her hair off. But prior to that, all sisters have to be completely pure. The dark curls covering most private parts will stay, though. They are not allowed to touch themselves, even for grooming.

The father leader comes into view with a naked male at his back, following closely behind. I have seen him around the village. He is physically strong and does a lot of the hunting. I always wonder how they make the pairings. Does it go on looks, or do they decide eenie meenie?

"Tonight, we mate a new pairing in our village. They will bring new life, new blood ties and more importantly, the new pure generation."

The leader turns to her and grips her braid painfully. "Do you swear to serve your husband and stay pure in your physical life form on earth, so your soul will be received and allowed into the gods' embrace?"

She nods once and then gets on her knees. There's no emotion shown on her face, well-conditioned since the day she could walk. The father leader steps away from her and gestures for her new husband to stand in front of her. He lays a hand on her shoulder while he recites their bonding vows.

She slowly rises to her feet when he taps the top of her head. She angles herself over the timber frame and leans over. Her legs rest against the frame, so her ass is pointed toward him, in the air. Her legs are apart just slightly, looking like she is very relaxed. If she is nervous, no one would tell. If we could tell, we could never show that we notice anyhow.

The man at her rear starts to slide his hand up and down his cock, causing it to harden. He pushes the head of his erect cock against her opening and nudges it in. As he forces it in, he makes a deep grunt. I can't help but grimace when he slams it the entire way in so his hips slap against her ass. I know the pain she feels as the hard shaft goes against the friction from the dry vagina walls.

Her body rocks against the frame as he thrusts in and out of her like a savage on a dog's heat. I divert my gaze. I have no interest in watching and don't believe in such things they suffer pain for.

What does gauge my interest, however, is the intense stare from the father leader. He normally watches the ceremony taking place as that is his duty. But instead of waiting for the completion, his vehement eyes never stray from where I stand. I become uncomfortable with the freshly piqued interest in me.

I can't look away though, it's like prey watching its predator. Watching every movement so you know when you need to run or fight for your life.

A deep frown forms along his forehead and he raises his arm, scratching at the soft stubble on his strong jaw. I mimic the frown, wondering why I may have caused such a reaction. But as I give up wondering, and drop my gaze toward the ground, the large bulge in his pants catches my attention. His thighs shift, obviously uncomfortable with the new reaction his body is having. Does it feel unnatural for him to be turned on by the show beside him?

The ceremony is completed with a final loud groan and fresh cum dribbling down between the girl's thighs as his cock is pulled out of her. Blood stains the tip and I swallow thickly at the sight. My body trembles as an uneasy shiver flutters through my body.

We take formation with our hands behind our backs, our cool hoods over our heads and we walk back silently, in single file to our quarters. My hand pauses on my door handle as I catch my brother in the corner of my eye. His expression is frosty, his eyes full of malice and I slowly open my door, knowing what comes next.

CHAPTER 3

I wait in the cabin, busying myself with some papers in front of me. Roughly putting them into an uneven pile, I stare at the wall opposite me. I try to send my mental and emotional self to the place only I am safe in as I count the small cracks in the old, fraying wood panel.

The door opens slowly before loud creaking on the timber floorboards echoes through the small space. The old wood groans louder these days, telling me that there have been many moons before me in this cult and many moons since I have been here.

My nails scrape along the benchtop as he creeps closer. By the time he is an inch away from my back, my hands are squeezed into tight fists, yet my eyes stay directly in front of me. I stopped looking at him a long time ago. He can't find me where I hide myself. He can never reach me there. There's a part of me he will never get.

He lifts my black gown, bunching it at my hips. The sound of the material rustling behind me does nothing to me. My heart rate is steady, my breathing even. Absently, I reach for the small jar of animal fat in front of me and slide it toward me. My brother's hand reaches past me and angrily grips the jar before he pulls it to his cock and coats his dick in it. Slamming the jar down afterward, his hot breath floats over my face.

"Stick your ass out, sister," he hisses in my ear, sending specks of spit flying into my ear. I back up a little and lean down over the benchtop. It makes it easier for me. Like I could give a fuck about how it makes him feel. His heavily booted foot kicks my ankles apart further and then he thrusts his cock into my opening.

"Black looks good on you. It's black like your heart. Rotten to the fucking core."

I exhale a long steady breath and focus on my herbs and spices across the room. I will have to grind them up and jar them tomorrow. My body rocks as he thrusts harder and harder, going as deep as he possibly can. The rosemary has really grown well this year. I will be able to dry double what I did last year. I smirk at the memory of watching the women shoveling sheep shit around the herbs while my ankle was chained, inside my cabin.

My head smashes painfully into the bench when my brother's hand slams down on my ear, holding my head firmly against the wood now.

"Oh that funny? You like it like this? You want me to ram it in your ass?" he bites out while holding his hard cock inside of me. It's pinned hard against my cervix, sending sharp pain up into my stomach. But pain is mental. If you have a strong mind, you can block pain out and it really becomes miniscule.

"I am happy about my rosemary," I say in a slow mumble.

He pulls out of me and flips me around so we are facing each other. This isn't right. This isn't what I want. I close my eyes, keeping myself firmly in my special place. The small corner of my mind that is safe from hurt and pain. I like it there.

"Open your fucking eyes," he hisses into my face.

I shake my head a few times not wanting to make eye contact with my brother.

"I will break you one day, Violet. I will break you, fuck you, break you more and then laugh while I watch you try to put yourself back together again."

"You will never break me. You know why? Because you may have soiled my soul and heart, but you could never ever compromise my mind or spirit," I breathe quietly with my eyes still closed.

He clucks his tongue and runs a finger down my nose slowly.

"Oh dear sister. You think this is as bad as it gets? I can and *will* break your spirit. What if I tie you down and satisfy you for endless hours, making you come hard for me over and over again."

"I would never. Not for you."

"Oh no you would. If I tease your nipples." He pinches both my nipples in between his fingers. "And then rub and lick this against your will, awakening your body and making it come whether you like it or not," he continues, rubbing my pussy up and down slowly.

"That would break you. Coming for your brother, coming all over my cock would ruin your spirit and poison your mind so you are never whole again," he barks before spreading my legs and lifting them over his hips.

I want to fight back but I don't want him to win either. I keep my eyes shut and stay calm. But my heart skips a dreaded beat and races a little faster now. He pounds into me while I show no emotion or thought toward him. It sends him into a frenzy. He thrashes into me over and over again before he finally pulls out and spills his cum over the front of me. He lets out a pitiful grunt before stepping back and putting his cock back in his pants.

"Next time I will come with rope and break you," he warns me and leaves. When I hear the door click shut and boots leaving my cabin, I finally open my eyes. I look down, candlelight from my lantern showing the blood streaks mixed in with the fresh semen. He hurt me bad tonight. But it's just physical. As I remove my gown and let it drop to my feet, I reach over and grab the arnica cream. I smother it over my vagina and slowly walk over to my small cot in the corner and curl up in it. I pull the wool blanket up to my chin and think about the first time my brother raped me. My virgin blood crusted at the base of his cock in his pubic hair, my endless tears falling onto his shirt. The inside of my cheek was ruined by my gritted teeth when I realized screaming was no use. He was angry as a teenager because he was a nobody here. He was going to be somebody in our village. Someone important on the council. *Here?* Here he is a nobody and they won't give him a wife because he isn't deemed pure by their standards. His resentment toward the only home he has is taken out on me.

Somehow it is my fault. But now, with the new threats, I am left feeling a new terror. Could he mean what he says? I don't want my body to be pleasured by him. I could never get wet by him so how could he force an orgasm on me? I turn over, willing the uneasy feelings to leave me so I can find sleep. My body would never do that for him. His threats are empty ones.

CHAPTER 4

With my white gown pressed firmly in the sodden ground from the weight of my knees, I listen to the morning vows from the cult leaders. The females are all perfectly still, trained and molded into the submissive race they have always intended us to be. Some of their values are the same as from where I was from. Some are not. The cruelties in my old cult were horrific and abusive—the lifestyle here is completely barbaric.

My tongue subtly peaks through the gap in my lips as I try to moisten them. We've been here for an hour, listening to the daily ramblings and village news. We are cold, damp from the morning dew, and physically worn. We all sit on our knees with our hands clasped in front of us and heads bowed. They are on the final vows. And I am glad because this morning's news was a long session and I can feel my body giving into the subtle tremor of tiredness. If it turns into an exhausted shake, I will get whipped.

"As god intended for our race, let us be the sisters' and mothers' voices. Let us be their eyes. Let us be their touch. Let us grow the last of the pure race." The father leader's voice booms around us. A male's heavy boots walk through the aisle behind me. Soft soil makes squishing noises under his weight. But the weight of the man's eyes and judgement is much, much heavier.

As the boots slow behind me, I know who they are paired with. Jeremiah.

He is one of the soldiers that is always at the forefront of the punishments handed out. He has a severe brutality about him. When he looks upon you before lashings, you will feel cold to the bone. Because behind his green eyes, there is *nothing*. He is vacant, void of any emotion but working robotically as if the only thing he knows or understands is torture.

His boots come down, pressing painfully slow on my toes and the soles of my feet that are facing up.

His foot twists, burning the skin on my feet with every movement.

With one last sharp push on my bare feet, he removes his boot and keeps strolling. But not without one "Oops my mistake," muttered under his breath.

I ignore the shiver that runs up my spine as he walks further away from me. I let myself feel the restlessness of that uneasy feeling and ignore the physical side effects. I breathe in through my nose and out through my pursed lips as we all slowly stand.

No one really ever wanted us here. And when my father passed away from an illness many years ago, they made it clearer that they saw us as trash. We were children, but still left alone in our one-bedroom cabin. Some nights we were both locked away and forgotten about so we wouldn't get dinner, and we would piss and shit in whatever bucket we had nearby. But Jeremiah? He hates me to the core. With every tiny cell in his body. If he could get the green light to torture me and cut parts of my flesh off, he would without hesitation whilst he danced along to the sound of my screams. If the original leader from when I first arrived was still alive, he would give him the green light. He used to allow Jeremiah to break my nose if he thought I looked funny. His son, the new father leader, took over when he died. And now he tells Jeremiah he can only punish me if I do something wrong. So Jeremiah always pushes me, hoping I will do something wrong.

We divide off as we busy ourselves with our daily chores. I am usually banished all day to my cabin, but on the off days, I can gather my herbs or wash in the river. The only sound we have is bird song from high in the trees that surround the village, a soft autumn breeze that whistles, and deep yet low voices from the fathers and brothers. While I position myself at the herb garden and look over the fresh sprigs I am going to take to dry, I allow my curious eyes to creep around the faces of women in the herb garden. I often wonder what their voices sound like. I have never heard them before. Are they light like mine? Or husky and deep? If they did speak, would their words sound obscured since they have never been taught to speak? Could they even make out anything intelligible or would it be strange sounds that don't make sense?

A cough sounds at my back and I jump. *Fuck.*

I was so lost in thought that my physical senses showed my betrayal of the rules. I don't dare turn around, so I slump my shoulders and snap off some fresh thyme before placing it into my soft sack bag on my waist.

"Do you want barbed wire across your back?"

It's the father leader's voice. Resisting the urge to look over my shoulder or react to his question, I carry on my task. One, two, three, I pluck three large bunches of rosemary and nestle them carefully on top of the thyme.

His fingers grip my arm painfully and I suck in a breath. He shouldn't be touching me.

"I think you would like it. You're broken aren't you, Violet? Your eyes stray too often and your words flow much too easily. You are meant to be shackled in your cabin straight after the morning ritual. You push the boundaries too far as the long days go on," he whispers close to my ear, before he walks away with his hands at his back. He wears loose linen pants and long sleeves. Yet when he moves, the fabric tightens around his shoulders. His hair is shaved, with just a light dusting over his scalp. He always keeps it short. His strong jaw and blue eyes suit it. But it also makes him look more terrifying.

He is due to be matched with a female on the next full moon. He had a female but she passed away shortly after their mating. She fell sick a few days after their ceremony and died within hours. Now that he's getting closer to thirty, the cult is becoming wary of the fact he is the leader with no mating and no offspring.

I leave the garden and make my way back to my small cabin. I find my string and wrap it around the base of the stems and then hang my fresh herbs from the cast iron rail that hangs from my ceiling. Wind rattles the old glass in the lone wooden frame, causing me to grimace. I don't want to wash myself with the brisk wind rolling through our valley but I have no choice. The sooner I can wash away my brother's resentment, the better.

"Give me your foot." A deep lethal voice catches my pondering thoughts. Jeremiah stands in the door, holding up a rusty key in his hand.

"I-I need to bathe," I reluctantly say. I tense, waiting for the inevitable.

Jeremiah closes the gap between us and back hands me across the face.

He squeezes my jaw tightly and brings us nose to nose. "I should let you stay filthy. Let your skin slowly rot from the grime all over you. I would happily watch maggots slowly eat you alive. Lucky for you, the almighty likes you around for your potion and preserving creations. Now move your fucking ass I have shit to do," he snarls then pushes me back painfully. My teeth ache from the pressure on my jaw but I refuse to show it. He will like it if I show him how much it hurts.

I leave my cabin and make my way through the trees toward the flowing river. Jeremiah's presence at my back, hot on my heels, is hard to ignore. The scenery around us changes slowly. Pine needles are replaced with rock crevices and large stones as the sound of running water becomes louder. A soldier catches my eye in my peripheral vision so I keep my eyes trained ahead. I don't want to be caught twice in one day with straying eyes.

Rapids rush by me as I turn toward the bathing hole. I'm not a lucky female that is mated in a cabin with running water. For me, I have to use the worn outhouse behind the communal room, a rusty pail that

I can empty in the morning and bathe in the river. Under normal circumstances, I wouldn't be allowed to wear my undergarments where people can see me. But I am a reject. Nothing on me needs to remain sacred in their eyes. I undo the buttons around my neck and tug the gown up and over my head. I chew the inside of my cheek as I resent the unflattering dress at my feet. I hate all that it stands for.

Without any more distraction, I turn and dive into the swimming hole. It's bliss under the fresh water. The silence pulls me into a comforting embrace. It's dark below me. I swim down further, toward the darkness and bask in all the relief my mind feels.

My lungs squeeze tight, protesting against the starvation they are going through. I swim up, breaking the surface with a loud gasp. I inhale and lock eyes with Jeremiah. He is standing on the edge of the water, holding my dress. His emotionless face on me is the only thing that scares me more than death. He is worse than death. I know that without a doubt. I float back in the water a little more, creating as much distance as I can. My sandy brown hair floats around me like wild arms reaching around for anything solid.

Slowly, he raises my dress to his nose and sniffs it, before he drops it to the ground and leaves me to talk to a soldier a few feet away. While they are in deep discussion, I climb out of the freezing water and drape the gown over my body again. I will wash and dry this one later when they allow me in the laundry room.

Once Jeremiah is done conversing, he shoves me from behind toward the small path through the trees.

"Just so you know, water hasn't helped. You still look and smell of rot."

CHAPTER 5

The next night the father leader comes to my cabin as I sit on the hard floor, mending the woven sack that holds my bed together. My brows furrow while I stay focused on my task at hand and thread nylon repeatedly through the small holes. I would love a mattress, maybe a fur throw in the winter, but this is what I have. I ignore the new intrusion in my small home. It's not surprising because my shackles get taken off at night so I can sleep. But my door gets bolted shut from the outside.

Silently, he moves closer before he crouches low beside me and wraps his rough fingers around my calf muscle. His touch feels like an invasion of my privacy. Which is stupid because I don't get privacy. But it feels like it is crossing a forbidden line that should never be crossed. He forces the key into the lock and twists as his eyes stay on my face, his breathing quickening. With a scrape, the lock clicks, and the key stops turning. The father leader slides the shackle open and pulls it from my foot before dropping it heavily on the ground.

"Do you like it when this gets taken off?" he asks me slowly while tapping a finger on the iron shackles with an aggressive manner.

I don't answer him; instead, I keep sewing up the holes in my bed. He grips my jaw in one of his large hands and pulls it toward him. I try to pull away from his agonizing touch but he squeezes harder.

"You speak a lot through your eyes. Do you even realize it? You frown, you squint, your lips smirk when you are thinking of something rebellious, no doubt. Your lips go white at the edges and form a straight line when you fight the urge to throw word vomit at who you have ill feelings for. As the decades pass, you grow lazy with hiding it. I don't know if you want to be tortured and rid of this existence, or if you are just plain stupid," he says quietly, watching over my face, searching it, every part of it, no doubt assessing the small details of change he speaks of.

"I want you to see what your future is if you let your untamed mind walk free," he growls low and lifts me under the elbow, pulling me up into standing position. The thick needle and nylon drop beside my toes as I raise my face in stark shock.

"You need to lock my door. That's the rules."

He clicks his tongue and sets his ice cold blue eyes on me with determination.

"You forget. Around here? I make the rules. I am the fucking god. Now move," he bites out and pulls me along and out of my cabin.

I am only in my thin gown, and it sways around my ankles as my bare feet meet the damp, dewy grass. My nipples harden as the sharp autumn wind caresses them. I need my hooded outer gown while I'm outside like this but the father leader doesn't care about that. He takes me past the community house toward the torture building. The lights are on in there. I can just see the glow of candles and lanterns through the cracks in the old, loose bricks. The shack is huge with a wicker roof and plane wood panel door. The size of it makes my stomach churn because I know it needs to be big to fit all the men in while they brutalize whoever their target is.

I try to yank my arm away from the man that pulls me toward the nightmare that I know awaits. But his fingers burn tighter against my sensitive skin as his grip hardens. I stare into the back of his head, forcing all my anger and revulsion toward it. I don't know why I fight the man in front of me, I don't know why I bait him with my loose lips because my entire fate is in his monstrous hands. Yet, I still berate him any chance I get. It is better when he leaves me alone. Being in his spotlight is nothing I have ever wanted.

The one thing that burns in my mind often, though, is the curious thought that may very well end my life—what is his birth name? It's been kept from me, from all the women. He was born as the future leader so as far as I was always concerned, he was the brother leader and now the father leader. I think often as to what name he would suit. But my mind comes up short.

I dig my heels in now that I can smell the burnt wax from inside the shed but it's no use. The father leader rips me forward so I crash into the back of him. He walks the last few steps, but he doesn't enter through the front door. We make our way around the back to where a small concrete water tank sits upon a wooden frame. The moss is barely visible under the moonlight that streams over the small village. The father leader pulls me beside the tank, grips the back of my head and forces it to look directly at the front toward the bricks. I understand now.

There is a gap. It's faint and wouldn't be visible in the daytime. But at night time with light on the inside of the building, I can make out the scene in front of me.

It's the woman from the ceremony the other night, with men surrounding her.

She has fresh fear in her eyes that nearly brings me to my knees. She was so compliant and eager to please the night of her mating. What has changed?

Her husband walks in front of her, holding the wooden bat that has barbed wire wrapped around the end. Tears stream down her cheeks and she shakes her head vehemently.

"I told you to cook me dinner. Instead, you got distracted and burnt my hard-earned venison steak to nothing but crispy charcoal. Despite what you think, I don't enjoy doing this. But never again will you be distracted. Your mind will always be solely on the task I give you. This is your duty as my wife." His voice comes out even, fixated.

He likes this. He wants to hurt her. Bile rises in my throat and I turn to the father leader with pleading eyes. For the first time I plead. I have accepted my fate since I was born but I don't want to see this. The fear in her eyes will haunt me until the day I die.

"I don't want to see this," I whisper with a soft tremble to my voice.

"Really, why do you think you ever have a fucking choice?" he grinds out in a hushed tone through gritted teeth. He squeezes the back of my skull painfully and forces my head back toward the gap. He doesn't let go, holding my head in a determined grip and leaning closer so he can look over my shoulder. His steady breathing brushes against my ear as I watch the men force my sister down and pull her garments up. Tears sting my eyes as I blink rapidly, sending them rolling down my pale cheeks. The contents in my stomach threaten to come up at any moment.

Her husband stands at her rear, while others hold her arms out in front of her. The thrashing begins and my stomach churns. She screams out, and one of the men grabs a linen cloth and pushes it into her mouth. Jeremiah stands off to the side. His hands are linked behind his back, while his attention is fixated on the scene playing out in front of him. His eyes don't stray, but his tongue runs along his lower lip subtly before he tilts his head a little. He loves this. I drop my regretful gaze back to *her*.

Her cheeks puff out and her eyes bug out as the scream she wants to let out is suffocated. Her face turns bright red while beads of sweat form on her forehead. I don't want to watch, but my head is still forced in place. I can't turn away but as the bat comes down and the sharp parts of the wire pierce the tender flesh on her ass cheeks, I squeeze my eyes shut and swallow the burning bile down. Something in me changes. My loud mind and curious thoughts become skewed with hateful malice and a new desire for revenge. Revenge for her. Not for me. I can accept my fate, but I cannot ever accept this playing out in front of me again. I slowly open my eyes and my full view is her husband's satisfied smile while he looks over the blood trickling down her thighs.

"Do you like watching her pain?" A deep voice is hushed against the nape of my neck. I forgot he was with me. The grip on the back of my head lessens and I turn my neck toward him. As our eyes lock, a deep, angry frown causes my brows to furrow.

"I want to kill him. I want to use that bat on his face," I hiss into his stern face.

"Dear Violet, keep up with the rebellious nature you have, and it may be your face being mutilated with the bat."

After I silently walk back to the cabin and get locked away for the night, I lie wide awake on my small cot. Sweat beads along my upper lip and my hair sticks to my forehead. It's the start of autumn; it's nearly time to light the fires. Yet here I lie with an uncomfortable heat radiating through my body. My hands are in tight fists that match the tightness in my stomach and heart.

If I wanted to, I could kill them all. Couldn't I?

The soft ember light flickers through my cabin. I allow my attention to roam over the spices and herbs in the glass jars. I have a wealth of knowledge now when it comes to natural remedies and food continents. But over my three decades on this earth, I have also learnt of the weeds and berries that humans should stay away from. The ones that cause painful deaths and debilitating illnesses.

A small curve forms on my lips when I think of the men that have caused endless pain, withering away on the floor, dying in a painful way. The fate they deserve. A new fate that I deserve. A fate for revenge.

CHAPTER 6

The weather is bleak outside. I place garlic cloves and dried lemon slices into a satchel before adding slices of ginger. I pull the string on it tightly and after a few loops, a soft ribbon is holding it tightly shut. Winter is coming, which means flu symptoms will start taking hold of a lot of people.

The first glimpses of morning sun attempt to break over the tops of the highest of trees but angry gray clouds hold it ransom. Rain belts against my window, which creates an even white noise for me, relaxing me as I make up another satchel.

Just as I begin to cringe at the brown lines under my nails from dirtiness, the lock on the door rattles. My chest rises, my breasts brushing my soft white gown as I suck in a deep breath as I wait to see who is unlocking my door and putting my shackles on.

It could be anyone. A job that is usually handed down after the fathers of the cult have their meeting. After last night, I don't want it to be any of them. A scene plays out in my head of them all dying slowly in the village, white foam leaking from their mouths as they struggle for breath.

Two cloves, four lemon slices...my hands work automatically as a deep yet well bonded evil settles in my aging bones.

The door edges open before it's forced the entire way. I might have to rub some venison fat on the hinges later. It is protesting more these days.

I can hear the heavy rain thudding down onto my timber flooring before the door is slammed shut. I don't look up. But I allow myself the reprieve of letting out my long breath as I relax my shoulders.

His voice echoes through my small room. An unhealthy shiver runs over my skin, leaving a pain of acid burning my skin in its wake.

"Maybe I shouldn't shackle your ankle today...you could try to escape and end up drowning in the river..." he huffs out as if he is imagining the whole tale of my demise in his head, and it makes him all too pleased. Jeremiah being anywhere near me makes bile burn in my throat. I square my shoulders; I won't let him scare me from my new path.

He walks closer to me. His breathing is loud, probably from running through the rain. Pussy doesn't like getting a little wet. He leans his backside against my wooden work bench and crosses his arms over his chest. His black clothes very nearly sway me from my task in front of me. My hands pause just briefly before I tie the bow and start on a new satchel.

"Oh, making your cute winter drink tonics. You're a good little weed, aren't you."

I grind my teeth together in frustration. I remember when we were little and he said Violets are an invasive weed and that's what I am. But he hasn't called me that in a long time.

"I might line yours with poison," I snarl before my eyes bug out when I realize what I have done. Jeremiah snaps and grips the nape of my neck painfully. He brings himself close to me, so close I can smell the forest on him. He's been out in the woods today.

"Oh how I want to cut the tongue from your devilish mouth. I go to sleep dreaming of it. Should I tell the father leader right now and have it done in front of everyone?"

My face pales and it angers me. I tell myself to be brave because they die or I die. I know there's no other way now. Going forward, it's them or me. Yet my body's reaction and natural response to fear doesn't match my thoughts.

"Make me one up, *Weed*. Make it a double dose because I should have a small babe in my house soon," he says with humor. He really trusts me to not poison it. Or is he humoring me and he will throw it out? Maybe he will test it on someone before he drinks it and then I will be hung in the trees for the crows.

I swallow and fist two garlic cloves tightly. "You're out of breath from avoiding the rain. I don't think there is a chance you will catch a chill, Jeremiah."

He lets go of my neck and throws his head back, laughing. "Oh you think I am puffing from running? No, we had a naughty hunter lurking in our woods, stealing our deer so I took care of him. Good workout though I must admit."

I frown and finally turn to him, looking him over properly. Blood specks are scattered over his nose and a small splatter up his jawline. The raindrops have mixed with the blood, now running down his neck.

The corner of his lips twitch as he fights a laugh from my reaction. He then pushes off the bench and crouches low, gripping one of my ankles tightly. "Don't worry, I cut him into small pieces with my axe and he will now feed the pigs."

I grunt and cover my mouth as fresh vomit threatens to escape my mouth. I swallow, fighting it as much as I can.

He locks the iron around my ankle and then runs a finger up my calf muscle as he stands.

"I'll bring you a pork chop on your birthday," he whispers against my face, then winks and leaves me in the cabin.

I lean on my forearms and heave air in and out as fast as possible.

None of them shall be saved. Some may just die slower than others.

My door is left unlocked, since there's no need for imprisonment now with me being bound to the floor in my hut.

The old, thick chain drags along the uneven floorboards while I re-trieve more bags to make winter tea. I have done this every winter that I can remember. The cult doctor treats everyone who becomes ill or has an accident. But I have always been made to make natural and holistic remedies. Anything around natural herbs, spices and remedies is my area.

Women will start coming to me for my winter tea. They know now that this entire bag will need to be emptied into a pot of boiling water and to be drunk over the course of several days if they start to feel a cold coming on.

In my opinion it tastes like crap, but who are we to have any opinion on it? I smirk to myself as my small jest.

The rain outside doesn't ease up. It settles in with the morning, looking more like a dark early evening. A small sigh escapes me when I think of my new seedlings that I didn't think to put away. They will be ruined by now. I could smell the rain in the air hours before it even started. The entire atmosphere changes when rain is impending. There's a soft smell to it, and the air gets a brisk coolness to it that differs from the autumn air.

The door rattles and two women burst through my door then politely close it behind them. They keep their heads bowed to me and hold out their baskets, waiting for me to give them the tea.

I want to talk to them. I want them to ask me for the remedies they desire. But everything is well-thought-out, including getting told seven days ago that the women will be tasked with getting their drinks today and I was to have them all made.

My desire to hear them speak, just once, or laugh with me over trivial things becomes more obsessive in my mind.

Roughly, I clear my throat and turn to grab the tea mixes. I take one in each hand and carefully drop them down into the bottom of their baskets. Simultaneously, they shut the lids and turn to leave my small cabin. But not before I catch a glimpse of the chocolate brown hair that peeks out of the bottom of the dampened hood.

It's her...

I touch her arm to stop her from leaving. When she jumps back and gasps loudly, I realize I have broken more laws. I grind my teeth together and hold my ground.

"I have some cream for you. That can heal your cuts faster," I say very slowly.

Both the women start shaking their heads and retreat further, nearing the door.

"I won't tell them. I can even help you put it on here," I insist and move toward my small jars of ointments. I find the healing ointment and place it into her basket beside the tea. "Please at least just put it on a few times. It will help with the pain. I promise," I whisper and step back until my backside is flush against the bench. She stares openly at me, head tilting to the side like she isn't sure if I am a friend or foe. She is thinking, being curious on her own accord. The other woman grabs her wrist and turns her toward the door before they both leave in a hurry. They don't bother closing my door. I stand there, watching them both run off through the rain toward their own homes. If the other woman tells her husband of our betrayal of the laws, we will both be killed.

CHAPTER 7

The rain is relentless for days. The sodden ground becomes a swamp infested with worms and loose mud. The father leader leads me toward the river where I will be made to bathe. I follow at a safe distance behind him, not wanting to be in his reach. His mood is off even for him. At first light he unlocked my door and simply said 'wash.' I would give anything for a warm bath. Like the cast iron bath I had in my family's house in my old village.

I may never know the reason behind the storm following the father leader. He trudges down over the rocks while I carefully step, trying not to trip and cut my feet up. Mud pushes up through the gaps between my toes as they sink down into the ground. I used to long for shoes, but now, as the rough soles of my feet scrape over a hard rock, I reiterate the fact that I now love touching the land with my feet. In summer, the grass is soft yet warm. In winter, it's wet and cold yet grounding. I can feel what type of day to expect from feeling how heavy or light the dew is on the grass. In winter, if the ground coverings have a frosty coating that chills my toes, I know we can expect sunshine. But most of all, the days I have the blessing of feeling the ground is a day I am not manacled to my single-room shack.

Today the mud feels glorious, because I have spent days alone in my cabin wondering if the men will be coming for me for what I said to the sisters.

While I look over the father leader's strong back that is hidden by his oil skin jacket, I smirk at the sadistic thought that at least I will be clean if they decide today is the day I die.

We pass by some of the guards and I force my eyes down onto the pebbled riverbed as we pass.

My brain has been humming with morbid fantasies of how I will take out the men that deserve it the most, but I am unsure on how the guards could be killed.

The rushing water flows past us as we pace to the water hole. I drop my hooded cloak and leave it on a boulder as I slowly take off my undergarments. The brisk cold air sends a sharp and painful sting against my hardened nipples. I don't look at father leader; instead, I turn and walk to the swimming hole edge. A misty fog floats through the air, creating a moody blanket. I raise one of my hands and weave it through the air, feeling the soft droplets of moisture lick at my skin from the thick air. I can feel his eyes on me. Does he imagine his hands around my throat? Does he wish he had his barbed wire bat with him so he could cover the sharp wire in pieces of my flesh?

I look down at the icy water, as if it is my safe haven. It is in a way. The quiet under the surface has given me reprieve from the horrifying emotions I am haunted with many times. I point my hands down in front of me and dive into the water. My skin sears with a white-hot burn from the subzero temperatures. I dive deep before I kick my feet upwards and break the surface with a loud gasp. Instantly, my teeth start chattering. I rub my hands under my breasts and between my thighs to ensure they are well washed.

His lurking gaze is still pinned on me. I bite down on my lower lip with a frown creasing along my forehead. I refuse to face him. He has watched me do this so many times. I'm sure he has seen my body morph over the years from a small child to the ripe age of thirty. But today his stare somehow threatens to warm my blood and heat my frozen skin. I feel a tingle between my legs and my heart speeds up.

I don't like this foreign feeling. This monster of a man will be killed. My body shouldn't be wanting his anger pointed toward me on my bare skin.

I turn but keep my eyes low and paddle through the water. I reach the edge and start to hoist myself out of the water before the father leader's boots are level with my eyes. He bends down and holds his hand out to me. *Don't take it, don't take it.*

I shake my head as my teeth chatter louder. He huffs and bends down further, wrapping his warm fingers around my cold forearm and drags me up. The front of my torso scrapes along the rocks, scoring my skin in its wake.

"Should have taken my hand," he hisses through his tight lips as his eyes linger on the bright blood. I creep past him and snatch my gown off the rock and tug it over my wet body. The white fabric clings to my skin, becoming see-through in my intimate places. I pull my hooded overcoat over the gown and stare at him expectantly. He needs to lead us back to my hut so he can chain my ankle once more. His arms cover his broad chest until he drops them and turns away from me.

He wastes no time in pacing past me, brushing my shoulder as he goes and heads back toward the village.

Water trickles down my legs and leaves my gown clinging to my torso. Goosebumps erupt over me as the wind whips across my moist skin and dripping hair. My long hair sticks to the sensitive skin on my neck while the tips settle over my round breasts. My warm breath swirls against the icy air, causing white clouds to flow in front of me, nearly touching the back of the father leader. We make it back to my small abode and I push the door open, heading straight for the ankle shackle. I want to be alone as soon as possible so I can get dried and try to escape the turbulent thoughts that took me by surprise in the river. But instead of the father leader hastily shackling my ankle, he pulls the door shut and leans his back against it. I watch him cross his arms slowly while his attention is pointed directly at me.

I frown deeply while my purple lips pull back and bare my chattering teeth.

Unable to control it, my entire body shakes and I hug my stomach, although it does no good with warming me up.

"I need your help." His deep voice vibrates through his rounded lips. He pushes off the door and stands straight as he pulls his oil skin hood away from his head. I look over his buzz cut head before I meet his cold blue eyes front on.

"Herbs? Tea? Ointment?" I murmur suspiciously. He normally demands what he needs from me and it is never seen as help or a favor.

"You know more than what you let on. You know how to heal people with natural medicine, but you know how to kill them and make them sick too."

I refuse to answer his accusation. I'm not stupid nor do I have a death wish.

While shivering and becoming dangerously close to hyperthermia, I stare blankly at him and keep my thoughts to myself.

"Then surely you know of other...remedies?" he says slowly. Very slowly.

"What remedies?" I ask, growing more curious now. Well if curiosity didn't kill the cat, then I may get my questions answered.

"Remember I let you speak, I let your eyes roam—yet you live," he says low and darkly. He's trying to reinstate his power over me. Remind me without his saying so, I would have had my head removed a long time ago. No one wants me here. I have a short rope, but it's still a rope.

"What remedies?"

"Be free with your tongue about my business and you will find hell has a special place for you. And I will be the grim reaper and Lucifer that serves all you deserve."

"What remedies?" I ask for a third time and narrow my gaze on him. He follows suit and stares at me with detached eyes.

"I want something to give me an erection."

A whoosh of air leaves me as I gasp. That was far from what I was expecting. My eyes widen and I clear my throat once I can breathe again.

"Ah—"

"Don't look at me like that or I will slice those eyes from your sockets. Try finding a way to shit and piss when you can't see and are shackled to the ground."

"I don't know of those remedies..." I say, growing panicked now. I could have utilized this, become indispensable to him and so I could get close enough to the men to get rid of them all. I could lie but when he doesn't get an erection, he will come for me.

"You have one week until my next mating ceremony. One week to figure it out. If I can't mate successfully with this wife, I may have to kill her like my last one," he growls and goes to leave but I stop him.

"My shackles?" I call out while he slowly opens my door.

"Call it motivation. Real good fucking motivation."

"What's your name?" I stutter.

He looks at me over his shoulder and glares at me for a brief moment before answering, "Phoenix."

The door slams shut as the wind catches it when he leaves.

Slowly, I drop my gowns from my body and they fall to the ground in a heavy, wet heap.

I have a lot to unpack right now. He can't get an erection. He can't mate. He killed his first wife. I can use the remedy to my advantage.

I stare at the closed door.

I've seen him with an erection though.

CHAPTER 8

I watch the red ginseng boil in the small saucepan above my cast iron cooktop. I stoke the fire under it before placing the rod against the wall. I run my fingers over my lips with my attention on the bubbling water that has an entire root bobbing up and down.

I don't know what the right dosage should be and I don't know if this will work. I heard whispers from the elders when I was younger, saying they would prepare this before mating was expected. Looking back, I can see the secret society had a large web throughout our home. There were looks, whispers, secret meet-ups. A man called Luca who was an outcast like I am now always promised me he would make sure I was safe. He always watched over me from a safe distance. Until the day they all escaped and I didn't. I used to wonder if he would come back for me. Though after fifteen years, I no longer have the urge to ponder. But I do wonder if there's a secret society here that whispers in the shadows, breaks the laws and longs for a different life. If there is, I haven't seen it yet, and now I am glad that I was trusted by my old family to know all these extra remedies and concoctions.

I take the saucepan and place it on the stone to let it cool off. While I brush my fingers through the long strands of my hair, I battle frustration that Phoenix hasn't been by for a trial run. His ceremony is tonight and if he can't perform, I have no idea what the outcome for him or me will be. His leadership relies on his ability to reproduce and people thinking he is the one the lords speak through and want on the throne. My life relies on this working because his anger and humiliation will be directed at me. But I also can't help but wonder what my life will even look like with a new leader.

There is a rattle at the door and soon after Phoenix steps inside. His serious eyes crawl over my small space before they finally land on me. My hand grips the bench behind me and I clench my jaw as I keep my focus in his direction.

"You really should have tried this before tonight," I murmur. He is in his black loose cargo pants, with no top and his loose black hooded cloak over his shoulders. The tendons on his muscles tense and bulge as he crunches his knuckles together. He is more on edge than what I could have imagined. Is he nervous?

The vibe rolling off him isn't one I want to be around. I can feel the intensity of it like I could feel molten lava burning my skin.

He steps toward me, his boots heavy against the timber flooring. A slow creak groans from the aging floor when he halts in front of me. He reaches past me, brushing my loose sleeve lightly as he stretches for the saucepan.

"It's hot and needs to be in a mug," I breathe tensely, staring ahead at his broad shoulder.

His hot skin is so close to me I can feel the warmth seeping through the thin fabric.

He brings the saucepan between us, hand tight around the handle, and sniffs the liquid. Steam rises between us, thick from the hot tea, but not enough to hide the brooding blue eyes that confuse me. Do they promise torture or hot pleasures? I swallow roughly, desperate not to gag on the big lump stuck in my parched throat.

Whatever his eyes may be telling me, it's detached and not a feeling he seems comfortable with.

My hips hit the bench behind me when Phoenix brings the saucepan between us and takes a sip. I'm scared it will burn me, but Phoenix isn't. He takes a big sip and then takes another larger mouthful. I gasp and watch his Adam's apple bob as the tea runs down his throat. It must be burning his insides.

Phoenix drinks more down before placing it on the stone. His face dips down, and I can feel his attention move to my breasts. He runs his hand up my stomach, over my hard nipples and over my bare collarbone. My skin ignites under his purposeful touch. His hands find my neck and tighten around it. My airway is cut off as he tightens his long fingers around my soft skin. I smack at his hands when my head begins to become light. The edges of him become fuzzy and I smack his hands harder.

"Never ever forget your life is in my hands. You living or dying is at the tip of my fingertips. You better hope this works," he says slowly into my face. His words are even. Not even a tremble.

He is confident. His words are entirely truthful.

The blurry edges become dark as I start to lose consciousness.

"You look beautiful with my hands taking the life from your body," I faintly hear the words. They sound far away. He drops me to the ground in a heap and steps back. I lie hunched on my side, wheezing in and out loudly. Saliva dribbles from my open lips as my lungs burn with the much-needed air inflating them now.

I look toward the door when I hear it open. Phoenix is hazy, but I can still just make him out. He grunts and looks down then back to me.

I can't make out his facial expression but I can feel the anger from him.

"Well, it looks like your drink worked," he bites out and slams the door behind him.

He hasn't asked me to come to this ceremony and I am glad.

I don't want to be anywhere near these vile creatures. Tears stream down my cheeks as I curl into a tight ball and stay on the floor. *I pray the crows feast on your flesh one day soon...*

I doze on and off while my fingers stay lightly wrapped around my own neck. The skin is bruised; I can feel it without even having to look at it.

My door opens and I slam my eyes shut while the tender flesh on my neck burns from my muscles tensing.

*It didn't work...*My only regret will be that I couldn't take some of them before my time was up.

My brother's voice fills the agonizing silence. I curl my knees up to my chest. It's not the voice I expected. But one I equally dread. I don't know if I am strong enough tonight to take my mind to that mental void of nothingness. The safe place he can't reach me.

He always seems to visit me straight after mating ceremonies. I always thought it was purely from resentment. But is he riled up and horny as well? I keep my eyes shut while swallowing the fresh bile that stings the back of my throat.

Let yourself go, Violet. Go to where you know no one can touch you. They can't break you if they can't have your spirit.

Slowly, I open my eyes and make eye contact with him.

I stay on the ground, not bothering to move. He can take what he wants and then fuck off.

But the smirk that pulls at the corner of his lips leaves me feeling ice cold.

"Oh not tonight lil' sis. You don't get to switch off. I told you there is worse out there..."

He gets on his knees and pushes me onto my back. My shoulders slam against the wood as he hovers over me.

"I told you I can force you to enjoy it. You thought it was so clever shutting yourself off from me so I was pretty much fucking a corpse. But you see? You need to hate what I give you. That's what turns me on more. I need you to see me as the devil and you're in hell," he whispers the last part as he pulls a small blade from his waistband.

His hand flicks across my stiff thigh as he tries to find the hem of my gown. He grips it and lifts it in the air, before he stabs the tip of the blade through the material. With a fast ripping sound, he drags the blade the whole way through it, right up to my chest where the gown finishes.

It falls away, fluttering down either side of me.

"Please don't do this," I beg him.

His smirk morphs into a large grin as he looks down over my naked body. Does he see I am far too thin? Does he see I haven't washed in days?

When my attention draws to his crotch and I see the mound under his pants, I cry. No, all he sees is his victim he needs to dominate.

I quickly throw myself into a roll sideways, desperately trying to get away from him. If I scream for help, no one will even want to help me, but they sure will kill my brother.

However, he is too fast and he grips my ankles and pulls my legs out from under me. I land on the floor painfully, falling back and hitting my head. My head spins and I feel blood trickle from it. Gingerly, I reach up and touch the gash on the back of my head and look over the vibrant, fresh blood on my fingertips. My brother comes over, grips my wrist and pushes my fingers into his mouth. He sucks the blood off before releasing my fingers again.

"Try to run again and I will cut your head from your body and I will quite literally fuck a corpse."

He teases my nipples with his fingers, pinching them and rolling them around. There's a sharp jolt through my body as he works them over and over.

I grab his forearms and sob loudly. But all he does is cluck his tongue and use his knee to open my thighs.

"What's the matter? Can't drift off? Can't stare off into space with those dead vacant eyes of yours?"

I don't reply. Instead, I turn my head and look at the far wall. But as much as I will it, he's right, I can't go to my safe space. His fingers tease and massage the sensitive parts on me that force my body to betray me. Betray everything it knows is wrong, yet feels right.

"I don't want this." My voice trembles as my harsh sob follows.

His fingers float lightly over my flat stomach, skimming my bony hips before he slips them between my wet lips. He rubs at my clit. I look up into his face and no longer see my brother at all. I see a monster. Another monster that shouldn't have the right to breathe.

His fingers slip inside of me and his breathing becomes more rapid. His fingers stretch against the inside of my pussy, dominating me in a way even my nightmares can't fathom.

"So wet for me. Does that make you angry? Does that make you feel sick? You should feel sick. You're not right in the head, Violet. Never have been," he says tauntingly.

Slowly, he drags my wetness up between my lips and rubs it over my clit. He rubs it in small circles while bending down and taking a nipple into his mouth.

My goddamn fucking nipples are my weakness. White-hot pleasure rips through my body as he nips at the tips on my nipples with his teeth and rubs my clit over and over again. There's a new sensation building in me. One that feels good. Addictive. A build up that feels better and better with every rub. His teeth scrape against my breast and the pad of his thumb works my swollen clit faster. A whimper escapes my lips and I flush red, pleasure and embarrassment equally causing me to blush.

This is wrong. I don't want this. I try one more time to push away from him. I make it onto my side but he holds me there. His hand snakes over my hips and finds my clit again, furiously working it. He straddles my side and rubs his firm balls against the side of my thigh while he massages and strokes my pussy. His other hand kneads my breast and then his thumb and finger pinch my nipple harder. With a subtle twist in the hard grip, hot tingling spreads right down to my toes. My body becomes an inferno of building need.

I cry out as the pleasure becomes too much and a wave of ecstasy hits me like a tsunami.

A throaty cry rips from my throat, with regretful tears running down my cheeks. My brother flips me onto my back, nestles between my thighs and thrusts into me deeply. His hard, rigid cock thrusts in and out of me like I am the only meal he has had in days. He is starved. Crazed. He lifts a thigh just slightly, his fingers pushing into my soft skin. He grinds his hips against me, moaning in satisfaction when his cock is stretching every part of my vagina. He's never been this worked up.

I hate him.

I hate him.

He slams into me one final time. As the base thrusts deep, his hard balls slam against my opening. "Fuck…" he groans while his eyes flutter shut.

I push at him as his masculine body becomes heavy over mine from exhaustion.

"Told you I would break you." His hot breath is vile against my hair as he taunts me again.

CHAPTER 9

My cheeks itch now that my salty tears have dried on my skin. I still sit on the floor, unable to bring myself to sit on the bed. That feels too normal, too human for the deranged monster I now identify as.

The strong pungent smell of wax fills the air while my tea light candles burn low and dim.

While I stare off into the open space in front of me, I seek out a part of my mind that remains untouched. A part of my soul and humanity that I can cling to but there is nothing there.

I readjust my sitting position but as I reach up to scratch my cheeks, my forearm brushes against my nipples and I gag loudly. I swallow quickly, hoping the burning of stomach acid that now occupies my mouth will go away but the sensitive feeling on my nipples is still there. I lean to the side and throw up all over the timber floor beside me.

My fingers are splayed wide as I lean on my hands, praying I still have the physical strength to hold me up because I certainly no longer have the mental or emotional strength.

My back tenses as another mouthful of vomit flies out of my mouth and adds to the impressive puddle.

I lean my head back against the cabinet and wipe my mouth with the back of my hand. A pained wail escapes me when the traumatic memories refuse to leave me be. They haunt me, the uncontrollable moans and erupting climax forced upon me makes breathing now seem unbearable.

I look down, agitated from the flicker of shadow from the candlelight that dances over my ample breasts. I used to like the roundness of them, the perky bounce when I walked. The one bonus of never bearing children. Now I realize they are a weapon. A weapon my brother can, and most likely will use against me again when he feels the need. Staying where I am, I reach above my head and feel around the bench. My hand slaps the surface before it begins blindly searching for my knife. I know it's up there. I used it to cut straining muslin cloth earlier.

My fingers land on it so I wiggle them until my fingers are wrapped around the handle. I bring it down to me and turn the blade over so the shadows now dance on it. This brings me more joy. The thought of wielding another weapon of my own. One that can also be used in my defense.

I chew my cheek as I rub the sharp tip of the blade over my nipples. My sandy brown hair drops over my bare breasts and without hesitation, I flick my hair over my shoulder with the knife. Slowly, I run the blade over my breast again, pushing firmer on the outside of my nipple. A tiny pinprick of blood licks at the tip of the blade. I smile at the new pain, watching the blood closely. *It is almost like it is giving it the kiss of death.*

On a breath, I dig the blade in deeper and grip under my breast with my other hand. I drag the blade around my areola and I'm not gentle about it. I don't have time to be gentle. I need them gone. Blood pools in my mouth as my teeth pierce through the side of my cheek I insist on using as a gag. Tears drip on my chest and roll onto my bleeding nipple as I slice the blade around the entire nub. With a shaking hand, I pull my nipple out and then quickly push the blade through the flesh, severing the last of it from my boob. I drop it to the ground with blood now pouring down my stomach.

Don't be a pussy, Violet. He can never use your nipples for his greed again! I scream internally at myself.

"Goddamn!" I hiss through my teeth as the knife blade rattles against the floor from my trembling hand that still grips it.

With a shaking hand, I grip the tip of my other nipple. I don't have time to be *clean* right now. The pain and blood loss is making me feel faint. I slice downward, but it's not neat and tidy. The skin is tougher to get through this way. I push the blade backward and forward with as much pressure as I can.

Ahhh! My self-inflicted pain and frustration roar out of me in a loud scream. No self-made gag could keep me from feeling every bit of this pain.

The knife hacks through the last piece of nipple flesh and I throw it beside me, making it land right next to the other sliced flesh. My body begins trembling uncontrollably. The knife slips from my fingers with a rattle as it meets the ground. I pant rigorously with whimpers in between as I lie on the floor.

I close my eyes and will myself to just sleep. Maybe when I wake, the pain will be better. Or I won't wake up at all and the pain will be even better.

Begrudgingly, I force my eyes open, but they refuse to cooperate any more than tight slits. A lone figure steps into my once peaceful cabin and stomps toward me.

The smell of moss and sweat fills my senses as the figure kneels close to me. I know my eyes are swollen, because exhaustion aside, I really can't open my fucking eyes wide enough to see their face. I can only assume I know who it is. Ripping of fabric follows before cool material is placed over my mutilated breasts.

"You can never taste my nipples again brother..." I mumble. The figure's hands still and a warm huff of breath brushes over my face.

After a brief moment, the material is fastened tightly around me and I am lifted up, cradled against a hard chest. I know, because I can hear the thunderous heartbeat in my ear.

I'm laid down on what I can only assume is my cot. I turn to the side and pull my knees tightly against my stomach, careful not to touch my burning chest. The pain is a lot now. It's getting worse before it gets better.

I am left alone, the cabin door slamming shut. I drift off. I don't know how I can, but I do.

I don't know how much time passes, but I wake in pitch black. My candles have burnt out. A strong hand grips my jaw and pries my teeth apart. I turn my head away but the strong grip forces it open to him again. I feel two small tablets slip onto my tongue before my chin is pushed up, shutting my mouth firmly.

"Swallow them. Next time try cutting your brother's body parts off instead of your own," a deep gravelly voice bites out. Boots thud against the ground and the door is slammed shut again, this time getting locked afterward. I swallow the pills, my throat struggling because I am so thirsty.

I force my eyes shut, wondering who the man is because it certainly wasn't my brother.

The fabric around my mangled breasts is soaked with blood, but I can feel when the bleeding begins to slow. When I have more strength in the morning, maybe I will try and stitch them up.

CHAPTER 10

The tips of my pale fingers burn as I scrape ice from the frosted ground. I work quickly, even though my entire body trembles with overwhelming pain. *I don't know if I want to vomit or faint*, I think to myself as I hastily throw as much frosty floor coverings and dew into the small jar as I can. I turn on my heels and pace back to my home, throwing the door open and kicking it shut with my foot. I let out a long, steady breath as I sit down on the edge of my bed, ignoring the withering creek the wooden frame gives me.

Before the ice particles have a chance to become warm and melt, I drop the gown off my shoulders, exposing my bandaged breasts. I unravel the fabric, hissing loudly when the last part sticks stubbornly to my wounds. Tears blur my vision and roll down my cheeks as I procrastinate. Sniffing loudly and blowing out through my pursed lips, I pull the makeshift bandage off.

"Ah fuck!" I grind out before I double over and vomit all over my feet. Sweat beads along my forehead as I feel my face pale. *In through my nose and out through my lips*, I keep repeating in my head while my vision blurs.

I sit up slowly and grimace as blood trickles down my stomach. I shake the jar a little so icy coverings land directly on the open wound. I repeat the process on the other side. The coolness soothes the burning pain I've been feeling since I cut them from my skin. I lie back, flat on my back so the frosty coverings have a good amount of time to numb the skin. Turning my head slowly, my eyes meet the sharp needle and thread that sits at the head of my bed. *It'll be worth it...*

The door edges open and boots thud on the ground. I freeze, knowing I have no way of being able to hide the mutilation I have bestowed upon myself. A slow, continual creak is the only noise to be heard in my small space. I scrunch my hands into tight balls while waiting for the scorning and lashings. Instead, deep breathing intensifies as the new occupant nears my cot.

A shadow casts over me and Phoenix drops to his knees with a thud. As the words leave his mouth, I frown. "I would have taken pleasure in taking your skin from your flesh. Instead all I see is this fucking mess. Who did this to you?"

His words are clipped while his eyes assess the mess. I can only imagine what is running through his mind when he sees the melting frosts covering the floor. I see no point in lying. *Let the pine needles land where they fall*, I inwardly amuse myself. I brush my wounds off and bite down on my lower lip.

"I did," I admit once I can form coherent words.

His eyes pause for a lengthy amount of time. The stillness of him now makes me squirm. How does his steel sharp eyes floor me more than the actions he possesses with his hands?

His hands move slowly, hovering over my breasts, but never touching my skin. I can feel the warmth of his hands but not the feel of his skin against my own. As his brow settles above his eyes, I see the confusion finally seeping through his sober persona.

"Why?"

The single word sends a spooked quiver through my body as my brain settles on the memory of my brother basking in my pleasured whimpers, the regretful tears and the wetness between my legs that made me feel like a sick monster.

I swallow and finally turn my head so our eyes meet.

"Because I am powerful and I took my power back. If I have a weakness that can be exploited, I will take it away. You can never make me feel like a lesser person than you ever again."

His hands finally make contact with my skin when he grips my chin and presses the pad of his thumb painfully against my lower lip. He draws it down slowly, showing my teeth. Instinctively, I try to pull away but he holds me in place. He bends down, lowering his face over mine so my view is filled with his face. His ice blue eyes bore into me, making me feel small and insignificant. I can't let myself feel like this anymore. I told myself I wouldn't.

"You have no power here. You breathe because I say you can breathe. You remain unchained because I say so. You fucking wash that cunt of yours in the river when I allow it," he says so quietly I wonder if I imagine his lips moving at all. "Tell me, how did your skinned nipples become a problem for you?"

He lets my lip go so I can speak. I lift my chin just slightly, feigning confidence and rebellious behavior. *Fake it till you make it.*

"My brother enjoys his private time with me and nipple play is his favorite pastime. So I simply took them away."

He straightens, but still hovers. A thoughtful expression crosses his face as he tilts his head and looks at me. I don't know what it is exactly, but it feels like he's looking at me in a new light. He clears his throat and says, "Simply."

I scrunch my face up. Well it seemed simple to me. Wouldn't anybody do the same in my position?

His arm reaches over me and snags the cotton and needle. I sit up and shuffle back so my back is against the frail wall. He climbs onto my cot, facing me.

"I will do that."

He shakes his head slowly and then arches a brow at me. "No, I think you have messed yourself up enough, don't you?"

"Won't you banish me to death and torture me for this?"

"I should," he agrees but says nothing more. He gets up and walks across the room, looking over my jars on the shelf.

His fingers glide over the labels I have created before he finds the antiseptic ointment and pulls it from the shelf.

He returns to me and drops the jar beside me before sitting back on the cot.

"I could make you pass out for this. It would be kinder."

"Are you capable of showing kindness?" I throw back at him. Why am I baiting him? I think my nerves are deflecting into anger.

His lips twitch at the corners and he smirks while holding one of my torn rags over my nipple.

"I show you too much kindness," he bites out, wiping the rag over the raw wound. I scream out and he pushes his free hand over my mouth while he wipes the other one clean. Tears stream down my cheeks and my eyes widen with the new pain.

Once he is done, he removes his hand and picks up the needle, carefully putting the cotton thread through it.

"This is going to hurt like a bitch. Put a rag in your mouth," he warns me. I don't hesitate. I stuff as much as I can into my mouth. The frosty ground coverings were fruitless. They were not enough to numb the area at all.

He holds my breast with one hand and presses the tip on the needle against a piece of my flesh. I start to tremble, then I look down and see how hard he is. He's enjoying this?

Confusion envelopes me and I look up to meet his hungry gaze, just as he pushes the tip through my skin. I scream into my gag, making unintelligible noises. His grip on my breast grows firmer, holding me tightly in place. The thread runs through the small hole before he pushes the needle through the other side. I start choking and pray to whatever gods could be listening that I pass out from the pain.

CHAPTER 11

The coming days have been a mixture of pain and confusion. Phoenix and Jeremiah have stayed close to my hut and every so often I will glimpse them out my window. They always side eye me as if they can feel the weight of my stare on them. At night, I watch out the window at their ceremonies; at mornings, I stare at their morning rituals. But as of yet, I haven't been asked to attend anymore. Last night, an antibiotic and painkillers were put at the foot of my bed while I slept. I'm starting to wonder if it is my brother and the guilt from what he did to me is eating away at him. Is he feeling what having a conscience is for the first time?

By the fourth day, as the sun sets behind the tall trees, I am collected by Jeremiah. I bow my head, curl my shoulders in like I have many times before and wait on his instructions. I speak freely around Phoenix when I know I shouldn't yet somehow with the rest of the cult, I know not to push the laws they have bestowed upon us.

"Move, you're having dinner in the hall."

I pause with one foot half in the air before I catch myself and fall in line once more behind him. He leads me silently to the communal hall and I become more wary the closer I get. I don't eat here with everyone. Is this a setup and I will finally be slain?

We both walk in, with everyone else already seated. The women sit silent with their hands placed neatly on top of the other, palm down and flat on the table. Their white gowns are still as they hold themselves like statues, eyes diverted downward.

The men eat, loud and fast. The small boys giggle and hold immature conversations but the small girls look dull, sad and forgotten. My heart breaks for them. Because I see myself in them. How can this life be right? How can they think being this submissive is God's work?

Jeremiah kicks my feet out from under me, making me fall against the wooden bench seat. His hand comes down across my face an instant later, rattling the teeth. Out of human reaction, I cup my stinging cheek with my hand while my eyes water.

"Sit in the fucking seat and keep your fucking eyes to yourself," he growls down at me as he looms over me. I struggle to get off my knees and slide onto the seat. But I do it and place my hands flat on the table, copying the other women.

Jeremiah is my shadow behind me, not eating but guarding. He takes his job seriously. Being the lead guard means he handles all security and obviously me.

Phoenix is across the table two seats up, next to his new wife. I don't risk looking up again. I can feel the heat on my skin from the fresh bruising but I don't risk rubbing it to try and sedate the pain.

I focus on the grooves in the wood table. The timber is old, but beautiful. I'm sure it's one of the original furnishings created here. Some areas look almost matte from where the varnish has worn away. The knots in the wood create dark-lined patterns.

Five minutes later, Phoenix clears his throat and holds his hands out in front of him. My head is low but I'm peeking up through my eyelashes. My stubborn curiosity deserves a slap from myself. I wait for the other women to lift their knives and forks and start cutting into their boiled potato and venison stew dinner. I look down to mine and once I have picked up my fork, I flick the meat around with the thongs. A piece of tender steak falls apart. Normally when this gets delivered to my cabin late at night as an afterthought, it's cold with fat dried on top, but tonight steam rises from the food, enticing me to scoff it. I carefully scoop up some meat, with gravy dripping off onto the porcelain plate. It melts on my tongue when I place it into my mouth.

As I swallow it down, I sneak a glance at Phoenix. I can feel his eyes on me; it pulls my attention to him. He watches me eat another mouthful and I frown then dip my attention back to my food. I'm the most uninteresting person here so why the fuck does he keep staring at me?

I slice into a potato then place a small piece in my mouth. As I begin chewing, I hear a choked garble before the commotion around me erupts.

I can't help but look up toward the sound. It seems like a natural response given what is happening. Yet other women simply stand and move out of the room in single file. Is this normal for them? Have they experienced this before?

I stay seated and tilt my head in the direction of Phoenix's wife, whose face is now slanted.

Her cheeks are bright red while her eyes bulge big and wide.

"Someone help her. Where's the doctor?" Phoenix demands loudly, yelling the building down. He is frantic, scared. Maybe he does have a heart after all. The doctor rushes to her side and smacks her on the back a few times. Her small, young hands come up and she grips herself around her throat. I can't stop staring, helplessly watching her struggle to breathe. Moments later, she slumps forward and her head smacks down onto the table. Her open, lifeless eyes haunt me.

"Why? Lords, why do you take another wife from me? What message do you try to send me?" Phoenix gasps, looking toward the ceiling as if someone will actually answer back.

Finally, he looks down and brushes a tendril of her hair away from her still face. "May the lords allow you into their warm embrace," he whispers and then nods to Jeremiah, who still stands behind me.

"We will send her physical body back to the gods tomorrow night. Make sure the women clean her well in the morning." He makes his orders clear. Jeremiah grips the back of my neck, giving me a fright and reminding me that I broke the rules again. He tugs at my neck, forcing me to my feet.

"Get back to your cabin, law breaker," he growls at me. But I wonder if him berating me is becoming almost a game to him now. Like I am a toy.

I slip past him once his grip loosens and I head toward the door.

"By lords, I really have no luck with my wives," Phoenix grumbles. I glance over to him and frown then choke when I am met with a wink. *He winked at me.* I suck in a breath and rush through the threshold of the door and stomp toward my home. I hear footsteps behind me. I know men would have been ordered to accompany me and lock my door for the night. I don't look back to see who follows. I feel physically sick. The cold air rushes against my aching breasts as I pick up my pace. I stumble up my steps and burst through my door before I slam it behind me. My back is pressed against the closed door as I slowly sink to the floor. I bring my knees up and hug them close to my chest, as much as I can without causing myself more pain.

Could he really have killed her? I think back to one of our previous conversations, where he mentioned he had to kill his last wife. I never pushed him on the comment because I didn't think he would literally do that. I hit myself in the head a few times. How could I be so stupid? I berate myself for the brief moment I thought he may have a heart and was upset about her death. A snort leaves me before it is followed with a hysterical cackle. He doesn't have a heart. No one here has a heart. Deep down, I truly believe even I don't have a heart. The demonic thoughts that caress my mind every single day make me believe that anyone born into these cults are born with no humanity. We are all evil, but some more than others.

CHAPTER 12

It's moody outside. Angry clouds linger just above the trees. The dark gray taunts me as if they are looking down at me and laughing about what is to come. I glare out the window while patting tea tree ointment on my stitches. I don't want to be invited tonight, but I have a sinking feeling the wink last night meant Phoenix isn't done with me and the game playing.

I glance over some of my jars and ponder which ones could give me an illicit high. A mischievous grin spreads across my face when I contemplate the possibilities of what could happen if I was out of it during the ceremony. I could giggle my way through the nastiness; I could be delirious and then pass out halfway through. The lashing would wake me up but at least I would miss the rest.

When I make the decision to try some out, the handle rattles and the door groans when it slowly opens. Phoenix comes in, dressed in black, ready for business. That's how I feel about this event anyway. While I cast my assessing gaze at Phoenix, I see a man that planned something lethal for his wife. A business deal. But I don't know the why's of it.

He saunters over to me, the hem of his linen pants dragging along the ground. His black top is loose, with a sharp, deep V shape cut around the top so his collarbone and strong chest is showing. His jawline has a faint scattering of regrowth that matches the spikey hair on his head.

"Didn't think to shave for the celebration?"

His lips open in feigned shock. "You wound me, Violet. I am in mourning and you mock me."

He is sick, evil and completely fucking unhinged. Yet being in his presence always fuels my unyielding personality. I step into him and run my finger lightly over his collarbone.

"Why take her as your mate if you just planned to kill her?"

In the blink of an eye, Phoenix snatches my hand and squeezes it painfully. But I raise my chin and hold his eye contact.

"Because I am a king that deserves a queen."

I scoff in his face, making him angrier. "You really think you will find a queen here? With women that can't think for themselves. You have created a subservient army."

He simply shrugs one shoulder and brings my hand to his mouth. He kisses the tip of my finger before dropping it so it hangs loosely at my side.

"Did you know I couldn't fuck her?" he says and tilts his head at me, gauging my reaction.

"I have a wee problem, you see. I can't get hard for these subservient women. I think you are the problem. You and your stubborn fucking mouth. Maybe I want your vicious teeth biting my hard cock. This is all a big problem. I don't know how to fix it. As if I could ever take a reject like you as my fucking mate," he says low, deathly yet his hard cock presses against my stomach.

I try to step away from it but he quickly snakes an arm around my waist and pulls me harder against it. It feels good but I will never give him pleasure in knowing that.

"You're broken. You are no lord of the cult."

"I know. Like I said before. I am the fucking king," he bites out and nips my bottom lip. He lets go of me, causing me to stumble back against my work bench. I suck in a deep breath as he turns and walks away from me. He casts a thoughtful look over his shoulder, toward me.

"Get your black gown on. You will watch my mate burn to ashes."

"Is that why you killed them both? So people wouldn't figure out you were unable to fuck them till they couldn't walk?"

The only hint I get that he is listening is his chest rising up when he sucks in a big breath. He cracks his neck from side to side and smirks at me before leaving.

***

Night time comes soon after. I walk toward the growing crowd, sucking on my top lip while I watch Jeremiah and a few other men add bundles of dried branches to the high bonfire. I can't help but scrunch my nose up when I remind myself that soon the air will be rank with burning flesh and ashy bones. Lowering my head and sagging my shoulders, I fall in line, mimicking the women's movements as much as possible. I haven't had much experience with these events, yet somehow, I am treated like I should be able to perfect every single part in this that is required of us.

A circle of women creates a ring around the bonfire, black cloaks matching the eerie dark night. Our hoods are raised high, with each perfectly pointed end high in the air since our heads are bowed. Our hands meet at our fronts, linked together and hidden in the long, thick gown sleeves. From the outside, we must look poetic. Perfect. Well trained. I know some of these women wear their physical scars on their backs and behinds as reminders of what happens when they are not perfect. I've seen many bloodied women and young girls carried from the torture shed.

"Kneel." Phoenix's voice breaks through the heavy silence. The woman next to him kneels, then one by one like a domino effect, we all kneel. The light dew from the autumn night soaks through the fabric covering my knees. The night is quiet, full of evil possibilities. Boots squelch on the wet grass as the males near, creating a larger perimeter around the outside of us. It's meant to be intimidating. To show their power over us and remind us who is boss. I imagine the women on either side of me filled with terror, petrified they will make one wrong move. I imagine the nearness of these monsters raise the hairs on the nape of their necks. Whilst focusing my eyes downward on the blades of flattened grass, I scrunch my nose. *Focus on keeping still, Violet.* My mind will never let me rest. Being a subservient with an obedient mind would be a fucking blessing at times like this.

There's new activity off to the side as Phoenix breaks our circle, walking toward the unlit bonfire carrying his wife's dead body. My weakness astounds even me because I break formation and look up at her. I gag when I see the state of her corpse. That's all she is now. Her skin isn't even pale. It looks more purple. Her eyes have tape over them and her lips are blue, cold and stiff. The back of my head burns and I cry out. Pain whips through my head like thunder cracking in my skull. I put my hand up to touch the back of my head but my hand is squeezed tightly from the back. One of the men crouches behind me, like a lethal panther.

"He may save your life. But we will always be able to destroy your soul, bitch. Fall in fucking line," he snarls. Instantly, my airways go tight and I grip my neck frantically. Rope is wrapped around my neck; it pinches my soft skin painfully.

"Next time you move your head when you're not meant to, I'll choke you to fucking death," he bites out then pushes my head down. Once again I look down, but this time I have rope hugging my neck.

The sound of branches snapping is loud when Phoenix rests the corpse on the top of the bonfire. The smell of petrol is strong, the fumes burning my nostrils as it's poured over her. *Don't cry, don't cry.*

There's something about the finality of the petrol, the reality that this is truly happening that burdens my heart. I didn't care for her, fuck, I didn't even know her. But this is it. She will never be seen again, taken because Phoenix said so.

I hear the strike of matches and then a *whoosh*. Heat flares out, and the night sky glows bright orange. The rope on my neck tightens when it is pulled back. "Now you get to watch her burn," the deep voice behind me snarls.

There's nothing but flames. A mountain of burning flames wood and one lone body that is swallowed completely.

A familiar smell fills the air. It's pungent. Rank. A smell you can never put into words. There's nothing like the smell of burning human flesh. I wonder if everyone smells it before they leave earth, or if *we are the only lucky handful,* I ponder sarcastically.

Do all dead people get sent to the sky in ash and smoke? Or do they do something different? I have always wondered what it is like outside the cult. The forest is safe to some but it's a prison fence to me. When a girl called Birdie was brought in from the outside world, she was so different. She spoke differently, and she kicked and screamed as if she thought someone could possibly hear her. But she looked like us. Men must go to the outside world when they get supplies but even with my keen ears, I never hear details of what it's like.

The smell grows stronger. It's offensive. My nose doesn't like it yet no one else seems to react. They all have straight faces, stripped of any emotion that would tell me if they feel anything like I do.

Not much time passes, or maybe it does. It's hard to tell when you have a rope wrapped around your neck and you're watching a body burning into nothing but bone. The bottom of the bonfire starts turning into hot embers and ash falls away from the fire, spreading across the grass. I look above the fire and see my brother standing at the back of the crowd. He glares at me, and his nose holds a deep wrinkle as he regards me with disgust. I can't help but smirk at him, with fabricated images of myself flashing him in my head, showing him my mangled breasts. Sure, he broke me for a brief moment, and then I took care of business and remembered I had things to take care of. I have people to kill. If I really needed to, I would cut off the sensitive part of my vagina if I ever thought he was going to use that to force pleasures on me.

My smirk angers him further. The corner of his lips turn downward and a scowl now occupies his normally passive face.

I edge forward on my hands and knees but the rope around my neck tugs backward, making me choke when it cuts off my airways. I sit back up on my knees after feeling like a feral dog that wanted to leap across the fire and rip my brother's head off. I lift my chin slightly and lick my lips while bringing my now soiled hands to the front of me, clasped together beneath my long sleeves. Let him come to me tonight. Maybe I will cut his cock off and preserve it in one of my jars.

CHAPTER 13

I touch the grazes on my neck, wishing I had a mirror so I could see the new bruising that I can feel beneath my skin. My candles burn bright in my small home as I use a wet rag to wipe my face. I can smell burnt flesh on my skin. It's in my clothes. Rotten and putrid.

The door opens and slams shut an instant later. I don't turn around yet. He can have my back.

"Washing yourself won't rid yourself of your sick little sins," he states, his boots scraping along the floor as he moves closer to me. I can hear him breathing. It sickens me.

I turn around slowly and smile at him. "You want some more of me?"

A deep frown forms above his eyebrows. "Remember how much you hated it last time. I'll make you want to hang yourself," he grunts.

I run a lone finger lightly through the crescent of my breasts. "Oh, you want my nipples again. You liked the taste of them? The way they puckered under your filthy little mouth, *brother*?"

I breathe and reach behind me, wrapping my long fingers around a folded old rag. I lift it up and raise it between us while never breaking eye contact.

"If you want them..." I open my fist, letting the contents drop to the floor. "Then fucking eat them," I snarl at him, feeling like a wild beast. His eyes leave mine and dip to the ground. His eyes narrow before they widen.

"What the fuck are those?" he asks me. I tilt my head and study the rotting bits of flesh.

"They are my nipples," I say, as if it should be obvious. They are wrinkled, drying yet rotting and the smell reminds me of decaying mice when they get stuck in my walls. I lean down and lift up the hem of my dress, raising it up and pulling it over my head.

He steps forward, his attention stuck on my new looking breasts. "You stupid fucking bitch," he growls and lunges toward me. He likes being in control. He likes feeling important. And I am the only person in his life that has ever been able to give him that since we left our old home. Now, I challenge even that.

He's stronger than me, and faster. I could never get away, so why bother trying? He throws himself at me, crashing the both of us on the ground. He straddles my naked body and slaps my stitches relentlessly before he wraps his hand around my throat. His eyes are lost, madness from being here has finally taken him as well.

Motherfuckers can't leave my throat alone.

Breathing is an impossible task now. My mouth is open but nothing goes in or out for that matter. I look into my brother's face, that unfortunately looks much like mine with his sandy hair and hostile eyes like Dad's. My ears ring loudly. I can't hear anything else. But Jeremiah's face appears over my brother's shoulder.

Without a second thought, he leans down and wraps his forearm around his neck and pulls my brother up. Choking him. I suck in a big breath and scramble backward.

"The only person I despise more than you, is *him*," Jeremiah says. He lets him go and punches my brother in the kidneys, making him drop to the ground. "Did fucking your sister make you feel like a big man?" Jeremiah taunts him, scaring even me.

"How did you know?" I ask. Jeremiah looks to me and raises his eyebrows in question. His attention falls to my bare chest but he isn't startled at the sight.

"It was you the night I did it?" I don't need to explain what I mean because all three of us in this room know.

Jeremiah moves his attention back to my face as he speaks. "I will give you two options. You can either kill him slowly, or I will kill him extra fucking slowly."

I look toward my brother who is still doubled over in pain. All I can feel is hatred for him.

"I think I have earnt the right to take his life."

"I let you talk freely to me this night. But don't let that tongue of yours get too loose or you will earn a spot next to him rather than in front of him."

My mouth closes sharply and I glare at them both. Never ever their equals.

"If you want to kill him this badly, get on your knees and say the one word with the most sincerity you can muster—please."

I can do this. For him. Not for Jeremiah. For my brother. To kill him. He is on my list. I can finally be rid of one.

I raise up to my knees and hone the perfect docile position that I have learnt from the moment I came to be on this earth. Our cult was different in some ways, but the theme was the same. Power over us all.

I hunch my shoulders, my bare ass resting against my heels as I kneel. My hair curtains around me, hiding his view and mine.

He bends over slightly and grips my chin painfully before he drags my face up so he is looking down at me.

"Oh no, you will look at me when you beg." His words are clipped, strained. My eyes dip slightly as his hard cock catches my attention now. Reluctantly, I peek back up to his stern face. His jawline as sharp as a knife's blade waits. A deep tingle settles deep in my stomach. He thinks he holds the power but when I see how his body reacts to me in my mutilated state, I can't help but feel something more.

"Please..." I whisper slowly. He grinds his teeth together but then his lips part, just slightly as his breathing grows heavy.

"Please what?"

"Please, I beg of you, *Jeremiah*," I draw his name out seductively. "Let me torture my brother and mutilate his body."

The tip of his tongue dips out, tracing the crease of his bottom lip.

"Tell me what you will do to him?" he asks. My cheeks grow warmer, a flush spreading up my neck. My own breathing becomes heavier. He is affecting me much more than I wanted him to. We are playing against each other now, a power struggle but who will come out on top?

"I will start with his nipples. Cut the top off each of them and then peel them back off his body. I will remove his fingers one by one, slowly for every time he has forced them into my dry pussy," I say and bring my hands together to emphasize my begging.

He follows the movement and then grips his cock through his pants. He squeezes it before shoving at it like he is frustrated by it. Angry at it, yet I thought men liked it when they got hard.

"How many times has he shoved his cock inside you?" he groans.

"Every month since my thirteenth birthday," I state, trying hard to not get sucked back to those horrid memories. It was so painful back then. It became easier when it stopped hurting and my mind could switch off.

"Then you should cut his cock off too?" Jeremiah asks and sucks in a breath.

"I would like that very much. Please," I plead again. My brother starts wailing and Jeremiah slams his fist down against his temple. He drops to the ground, dazed, but not unconscious. Jeremiah slowly begins pulling the waistband down on his pants. His cock springs free abruptly and I inhale sharply. It's so red and big. The tip glistens with pre-cum.

"You need to show me how much you want to be the one to torture him, Violet."

"Do I—do you want me to?" I stutter while eyeing the cock in front of me.

He drags a finger up my cheek and slowly around the back of my head, before he bunches my hair in a makeshift ponytail and fists it at the base of my scalp. "Don't be coy." His voice whips down at me, letting me know that right now there is no power play in place. He's the power, playing with me.

My head is kept tightly in place. Tentatively, I lift my hand and wrap it around the base of his cock. I open my mouth as he pulls my head closer to his cock. I put my lips on it and slide as much of his length into my mouth as I can. I pull back before I repeat the process. He pushes my head this time, making me choke and gag on the fullness in my throat. Eventually, he guides my head off his cock so I can take in a new breath. I run my tongue over the tip of his cock and wrap my lips around it again. I massage it with my tongue as my lips run up and down his thick shaft.

He's quiet, aside from his heavy breathing. I pull off his cock and look up to him. His eyes are closed, but he quickly opens them and frowns.

"Is that okay? Like nice?" I ask. Fuck, I hate how weak I sound right now.

"Have you never done this before?" he grinds out with flushed cheeks. I shake my head slightly.

He growls like an animal and rips my hair back so my back is bent savagely.

"Yes Violet, it is fucking nice," he says as my brother starts to sit up again. Jeremiah's leg raises and then he stomps his foot down on his head and holds it there, pinning him to the ground.

"Now fucking suck my cock so I can come in your mouth. But don't you dare swallow it," he bites out and forces my face to his cock again.

I'm confused but open my mouth and fill my mouth with his hard length. I squeeze the base as hard as I can and suck his dick like my life depends on it. My tongue massages as my lips glide up and down it. A groan leaves him and it cheers me on. It makes me move faster. My jaw starts to hurt, but I don't stop. I try something new and scrape my upper teeth lightly over his shaft.

"Just like that, Violet..." he groans, holding my head in place and thrusting into my mouth. Jeremiah fucks my face hard as he comes into the back of my throat. I remember his words and try not to swallow it down. He quickly pulls out of my mouth and then crouches down so we are on the same level. He drags my brother up by the collar of his shirt, fisting it hatefully. Jeremiah's smirk leaves me feeling so cold.

"Spit it into his mouth," he orders me.

I shake my head, the cum still sitting in my mouth. It takes everything in me not to gag and let it dribble from my mouth. Jeremiah grabs my jaw with his large hand and tenses while making his words slow.

Deliberate. "Spit it in his fucking mouth or you will share a box in the cold fucking ground."

He abruptly lets go of my face. I look down at my brother's frightened face. I haven't seen him scared in many, many years. I shuffle around and lean over him.

"Fuck off, Violet," he says in a rush.

Jeremiah laughs but it's not a nice laugh. A shiver runs up my spine as I grip both sides of his head and dribble Jeremiah's cum down into his mouth. He closes his lips but my work is done. I sit back and gaze up at Jeremiah's satisfied face. He pulls my brother to his feet and then stuffs his cock back into his pants.

"The night you cut those off..." He dips his head to my bare chest and slants his eyes while reflecting on the night. "I heard screams. I came in to join in the fun of torturing you. But I saw you passed out with a knife in your hands and your nipples missing. Then you mumbled something about your pathetic brother fucking you. That day you became much more interesting. You made me realize how little I like well-behaved females. Now you'll come to my favorite shed where we create art," he says.

CHAPTER 14

Small stones pinch my feet as I trail behind Jeremiah and my brother, who is still being dragged by his collar. It's dark out, and everyone is in their homes now. It's an unspoken rule that everyone is to be tucked away for the night before the start of the next day. Midnight.

The small, yet well-worn path winds through the outhouses and the vegetation gardens. I am careful not to stumble as we shy away from the light of the last wick in the outdoor lanterns.

Coming into view is the large shed. The same shed where I peeked through a small gap in the wall and watched a mated woman be beaten only a few nights earlier. Now, I will be inside the same shed doing the beating. Does this make me any different from the men in this godforsaken place? I still think I am.

Jeremiah stops at the front of the large doors and grips a handle, pulling it with great strength. The old door fights back against his force but it comes away and opens eventually. It opens enough for the three of us to slip through. Some more reluctant than others.

My brother trips on his own feet and stumbles when he hesitates in his steps, but Jeremiah pulls him forward hastily.

The shed is large, yet ancient. I can only guess that it was the first building that was built. It never stops groaning. Subtle but still groaning. The roof creaks as we make our way further in. Work benches frame the walls, creating a U shape with a lone chair in the middle with a large wooden pillar behind it. Restraints for those that stand, and restraints for those that are seated. It should sicken me, but I look around, intrigued. This is the first time I have been in this shed and on the other side of the situation. No longer am I here as prey; this time I am here as the hunter.

Dust tickles at my nose as I run a finger over some of the tools on one of the benches.

I keep my back to my brother as the sounds of Jeremiah tightening rope around him on the pole fill the once-quiet space.

"I will yell. I will fucking expose you for the traitor you are," my brother says to Jeremiah through gritted teeth.

"Screaming coming from this space isn't abnormal. No one would dare to come save you," Jeremiah says softly. So softly it makes his words sound more lethal.

"But in any case, so we can enjoy this romantic moment in peace," Jeremiah continues after a brief moment. Muffled groans and hushed screams follow, indicating Jeremiah has gagged him.

I feel him creep up behind me, the hard outline of his body pressing just so slightly against my hooded gown. I threw it on in haste so I am still naked underneath. He leans around me and lights a long candle with his own lit candle. He moves away from me in silence, lighting candles around the room. It feels icy cold where he once stood at my back. I chew on my bottom lip, hoping to distract myself from the odd change in feelings toward the man that has always scared me more than the hell everyone speaks of.

As the room becomes lighter and the soft flicker of flames flutter in the eerie night time, I turn around and face my brother. Jeremiah stands behind him with a satisfied look on his face while he flips a sharp knife in his hand, over and over.

"I guess you must feel right at home in here," I say and wave my hands around.

He grunts, covering his laughter. "Don't pretend this doesn't feel like home to you. You're just as fucked up as the rest of us."

"I'm fucked up because you and everyone else made me this way."

He shrugs his shoulders and runs his hand over the day-old stubble on his strong jawline. Some of his loose strands of hair are messy around his ears, the rest brushed back by his fingers at the nape of his neck. He turns his head toward my brother, creating a black shadow to drop over his profile. "Tell yourself whatever you need to."

I struggle to ignore my brother's tears that stream down both sides of his face. He went from someone that has held dominance over my entire life to looking like a pathetic piece of shit. Maybe I should end his life quickly and be done with it. I've never killed someone before.

Could I truly do it? I swallow and gaze over the tools around the room. *Yeah I think I could.*

I think of my healing breasts, the way he sucked on my nipples while he fucked me relentlessly. I think of the way he was mad at being a nobody, so he took his frustrations out on my pussy and ass. I think of the way I maintained perfect control for so many years, being a still body for him to fuck and tucking my sanity neatly away in the far depths of my mind where it was safe. I think of the moment he took that from me when he forced me to enjoy the sex with him. The whimpers that fell from my mouth when I enjoyed it even though I didn't want to.

I stare at him, in silence, for a very long time. I don't move for a while, until I eventually slip off to the side and grip a large pair of shearing scissors. My small hands don't seem strong enough, but with all my strength, I open and shut them a few times, satisfied with the scraping sound they make.

My brother starts to squirm in his seat, thrashing as much as the tight restraints will allow but it's no use. He's not going anywhere.

"Oh don't worry, brother. I'm not a savage. I will make you enjoy it first," I mutter quietly, thinking of the words he said to me.

I drop to my knees and crawl over to him, with the front of my outer gown opening at the front. My breasts becoming exposed as I close the gap between us. There is a tremble to his legs. I don't feel bad. I should, but I don't. My fingertips press into his knees and I pull myself up so I kneel in front of him. Slowly, I walk my fingers up my brother's thighs, and he tenses when I near his crotch. I don't think twice. I slip my fingers into the band on his pants and force my entire hand inside, searching for his soft shriveled up cock.

My fingers wrap around it, sliding up and down. The skin is loose, making it hard to handle. I grow frustrated and look up into his face. "You don't like me being in control? Is that it?"

"Dear Violet," Jeremiah chuckles behind me and places his hands on my brother's shoulders, squeezing ever so slightly. "You have a lot to learn about pleasure, pain and everything in between. Be patient, Violet. Think of him as your canvas and you are the artist."

I take in his advice and nod while licking my lips. Gingerly, I stand up and push my hand in further, gripping his balls. I massage them, rolling them in my hand. My brother shakes his head from side to side, whipping it furiously.

Jeremiah moves his hands so fast I barely caught it. He grips my brother's head firmly so he can no longer thrash about. "Don't fight it. Do you feel her soft warm hands on your cock and balls? Teasing them, rubbing them—making the blood flow right into the tip of your shaft."

I feel his soft cock twitch in my hand but it's still not hard. I wrap my fingers around his dick and rub it up and down, firmly, imagining myself pumping blood into it.

As if awakening from a deep sleep, it turns into a semi. I glance up, watching tears roll down his embarrassed cheeks. Jeremiah's hands run down over his collarbone and begin working both his nipples. His cock becomes solid in my hands and I swallow. My stomach begins to roll as I grow nauseous. Can I really do this? I have to! How can I move on until I have exacted my revenge?

I keep pumping his cock while grinding my teeth together. I puff my cheeks, feeling like a crazed lunatic. Jeremiah cackles while he pinches my brother's nipples and eyes the bulge in my brother's baggy linen pants. Will I become him when I am done? Will I find severing body pieces an exciting pastime? Most of all, will my humanity be lost forever and my curious eyes and nosey mind will be nothing more than a monster?

The back of my throat burns with bile; I swallow it down and raise my other hand. I tug my brother's erection free of his pants. As my hand glides to his tip, I quickly squeeze with all my might so it will stay in place. Without another wasted breath, I lift the shearing scissors and slice through his penis.

Muffled screams ignite in front of me while blood spills down between his thighs. It's bright, vibrant, full of life.

The pained sounds stop, only to be replaced by full-body sobs. His chest heaves in and out as a guttural cry erupts from him. I am surprised he isn't choking on the material in his mouth.

I run my fingers through the wet blood and wiggle them in front of my face, eyeing it intently.

"Addictive, isn't it? Powerful on a level that very few get to experience. Not many people get to play god, Violet. But here? We can. We can do whatever we want. Do you know how liberating it is sawing through bone?" Jeremiah says in awe.

A loud creak echoes through the building when the shed door is forced open. We both look toward the noise, eyes wide, wondering who may be disrupting us. Our eyes lock with Phoenix and a new shiver runs up my spine as dread fills my body. He is wild.

Chapter 15

"Pray tell, why you are both in here on this fine night?" Phoenix's voice booms through the shed. He paces toward us and steps in front of my brother. Nothing can hide the shock from his face as he assesses the scene in front of him. He pinches the bridge of his nose and sucks in a long, drawn-out breath. "And pray tell, why the *fuck* is his cock on the ground and no longer attached to his body?"

The heat I felt only moments ago has chilled, the blood in my veins turning to sharp ice.

My body stills as I watch Phoenix with a resilience I haven't felt in a long time. My attention on him doesn't waver as I lift my chin and show I hold no regret in my actions. My punishment will be worth it as far as I am concerned.

He clears his throat and stands over me. "Convenient. Now you have no words and become a perfect housewife when normally silence eludes you."

I stand slowly and step closer to him, my toes become damp with the blood that's now cooled on the ground. "He can no longer stick that retched thing inside of me. So, that is why his putrid cock is on the ground."

Phoenix's eyes slide down to the shriveled cock again, then slowly, he drags them back to me. He grips me around the neck and squeezes, just enough to make breathing hard. His other hand glides down my arm, gripping my wrist and bringing the blood close to his face. He bares his teeth, showing me how pissed off he is before dropping my arm.

"You are awfully quiet, Jeremiah," he says, staring directly into my face with a fierce venom.

"I'm not going to apologize if that is what you are after." Jeremiah steps off to the side. My eyes slide to him, watching him lean back against the tool bench and cross his arms over his chest.

"You could have punished him without her," Phoenix grills him. Jeremiah shrugs a hefty shoulder and tilts his head at us.

"She's fun. I'm fucking bored and sick of obedient women that don't fucking talk. Admit it, you like her for her loose tongue and fiery attitude too because you're bored out of your brain."

"She's not a toy. She could ruin everything our great-grandparents worked hard to establish."

"She could be our little secret."

I grow angry and sick of being a pawn in their cult life. I grip Phoenix's wrists and wheeze out, "Bite me."

Phoenix scoffs, causing his warm breath to wisp across my face. "Careful, I might." His voice becomes low, thoughtful almost. Is he contemplating me being a toy like Jeremiah suggested?

My brother squirms and cries into his gagged mouth, drawing all three of our attention back to him. Phoenix releases his grip on my neck, dropping his arm at his side and balling his fingers into tight fists. His neck tenses, tendons bulging, showing his frustration.

Jeremiah makes his way back behind my brother and claps his hands firmly over the side of his face. "Now what to do with you? You are a bad omen that cannot be sacrificed for the greater good. You can't be burned so your ashes float to the gods above." Jeremiah pats his shoulder and shakes his head, feigning sorrow. "No, I think the only option for you is to rot away in the ground and be nothing but an afterthought."

Jeremiah and Phoenix lock gazes with grim expressions before they both fix their attention back on me. I cross my bloodied hands across my chest before I quickly drop them and wrap my gown around myself. I forgot I was naked. How the fuck could I forget I was naked? My healing breasts must make them nauseous. I take a step back to create space between myself and the three men that have always been a nightmare in my life. But I don't back away to look scarce, no, instead I just create distance while I clear my throat.

"I know what happens now. I die. And to be honest, I have been expecting this day for a long time. But I have one wish before I die," I state and fall silent, waiting for one of them to answer me. They say nothing but Phoenix waves his hand in front of me, gesturing for me to keep going, while Jeremiah simply smirks at me like I am even more interesting to him now.

"Uh...Well...I want him to die before me. I want the satisfaction of knowing I at least outlived him," I finish and dip my head in my brother's direction.

Phoenix steps forward and rips my hands down before he pushes my gown apart.

"Your nipples used to pucker into perfect raspberries that begged to be ravaged. Now there are nothing but brutal scars in its place. Every time you bathed in the river, I would pray the cold water would make them stiff. I would pretend they were stiff for me," he says quietly, never taking his eyes from my wounds.

"I would tear my vagina off if it meant he would never fuck me again."

He raises his face from my breasts to my face, then slowly runs his index finger lightly over my lips before tapping on my pursed lips. "This right here is what makes me stiff. My cock swells painfully and my balls tighten so much, I fear I may die. Your strong will to ignore everything we say and hold dear in the cult is what keeps my hand fisted around my rigid cock at night."

I suck in a breath, parting my lips a little. That's all he needs though. He slips his finger inside my mouth and presses it down on my sharp lower teeth.

"Jeremiah wants to have you as a toy. A plaything. But I don't know if you can handle it. Maybe our game should be to see how long it takes to finally strip you of your strong will. But if you lose the fight in you, the rebellious side, you will be silent. You will be scared and so fucking boring."

He lets out a long slow wary breath. The sigh lets me know he is undecided. He is frustrated with the decision he needs to make. I guess at least I know my life isn't completely worthless. They think I am entertaining. I think of my time here, my life before, the life I ran from and the strong girl I once was in my old village. The strong grown woman I am now and what I have endured yet never lost my will to have my own voice. I bite down on his finger and then spit it out, scrunching up my nose.

"You could never beat me. I will kill everyone here, slowly but surely as long as you allow me to breathe. The day I die, I will die strong and happy," I state, proud of how strong my voice comes out.

Jeremiah's loud boots thud against the ground, growing closer to me. He stands, shoulder to shoulder with Phoenix, a wide smile stretching across his face. His eyes look mischievous, evil and fucking unhinged, but also delighted. I don't know what's worse. This level of psycho or Phoenix's heavy hand to have order over everything in this cult, including me. I look between them both, understanding their stark differences, seeing they want different things from me in one way, yet exactly the same thing from me in another way. I swallow and lick my lips, my throat feeling scratchy and dry now. Jeremiah wants to cause havoc with me; he wants to have me as his sidekick when he cuts people into pieces. Phoenix wants to own me, but have me as a secret. But without a doubt, they both want to fuck me, own my body and try to have power over my spirit.

What do *I* want?

I assumed without a doubt I would be dying soon. Presumably from one of the men in this shed with me. I briefly close my eyes before I slowly open them, sighing. I want to kill the man with the missing cock that sits before me and I want to kill every man that has beaten the women in this cult. Sweat beads on my forehead as Jeremiah bites on his lower lip seductively while Phoenix presses a finger under my chin and forces my face up further. The two morbid, broken men in front of me can help me achieve this goal and I may still be alive at the end of it. *Maybe.*

"She has tasted my cock," Jeremiah whispers, almost in awe.

"Did you like it, dear Violet?"

"It made me feel powerful," I admit.

"Did it make you wet?" Jeremiah asks with a raised eyebrow.

I bite my lip, diverting my gaze. I honestly don't know what it made me feel. Phoenix snakes his hand out and lightly runs a finger over the most sensitive part of me. A tingle spreads through my body, making my thighs quiver.

Phoenix inspects his finger and raises it to Jeremiah's face. "Mmm dry. I think we need to make you wet for us. If you want me to let you keep your torture night a secret, I want something in return. And that will be finally feeling your tight, wet pussy drenching my cock," he says, rubbing the front of my clit. His fingers spread my lips while he massages my swollen, needy pussy.

"Do you know what it's like to never feel a wet pussy in your fucking existence? The women here are silent, dry and don't moan with pleasure when we go balls deep. It's insane. Those women also make my cock so soft and limp," he finishes, continuing his rhythmic hand movements.

Jeremiah moves behind me and rubs his hands up and down my arms slowly, before moving over to my shoulders where he gently massages them. "So tense, wild Violet. We can't have that," he says after clicking his tongue.

My skin erupts in gooseflesh as a shiver spreads from head to toe. The tingle in my vagina grows and an intense need fills me deep in my belly. I've never felt need like this before.

My brother thrashes hopelessly against his restraints but it's not enough to make my mind wander from what's right in front of me. Jeremiah's glistening lips from where his warm tongue has just run along them, Phoenix's blue eyes that make me feel like he needs me right here, right now. Jeremiah's strong jaw, sharp like a knife's edge that calls to be bitten. Phoenix's strong hands, his precise finger movements, threatening to bring me to my knees. My body is hot and on the verge of combustion.

Phoenix presses a finger inside my pussy and grins. "So fucking warm and gloriously wet."

CHAPTER 16

Phoenix removes his finger slowly and reaches past me, pressing his wet finger into Jeremiah's mouth. He sucks the tip of Phoenix's finger, letting out moans of enjoyment.

"Oh yes, she tastes like honey and warm creamy milk," Jeremiah groans. His hands drop from my shoulders, glide down my bare back and cradle my hips. Phoenix nudges my thighs apart with his knee and locks eyes with me, drilling into me before he drops to his knees in one fast motion. His fingers grip my hips tightly, right below where Jeremiah holds me in place. The air has grown thick, heavy, with a tension that brings a promise of pleasure that is wrapped in dominance.

"What if I don't want that?" I say shakily, since I am trying to be strong and stubborn. But my words hold no strength with no force behind them. My words quiver as quickly as my pulse that beats too quickly.

I feel a rush of hot breath flutter against my damp lips as Phoenix lets out a soft chuckle, letting me know he doesn't think any part of me won't enjoy it.

Jeremiah presses his lips to my shoulder, planting soft delicate kisses to my skin. It's a contrast to how these two men usually treat me. I have grown to be scared of them, since they have never been kind. Now they are bored with their roles in this slower life that has fierce boundaries and I am their only form of distraction. As their entertainment, they will treat me just nice enough.

My body shrills with need and excitement, ignoring my wary mind.

The tip of Phoenix's tongue slips past his full lips and flicks over my clit. My thighs shake as my knees buckle, but Jeremiah holds me in place. His fingers grow tighter, digging deeper into my hips. This reminds me of his deadly strength and how easily things can change. They surround me, holding me in place, but not against my will. They are both in control, while my control evaporates through my scorching skin.

Without a second thought of my possible impending doom, a whimper leaves my mouth as Phoenix flicks my clit again. He swirls his tongue around in tight circles, which sends electric pleasure from my needy vagina to my limbs. My body becomes light and my head swims as the indulgent assault on my clit continues. I feel like the gravity has changed in the room and my entire body wants to float, yet the center of the pleasure is actually between my thighs. I never knew it could be like this.

I can feel fresh juices coat the inside of my thighs as it dribbles from my pussy while Phoenix focuses on the sensitive spot. His tongue swirls around more, making the movements purposeful and concentrated.

"Faster..." I whisper.

I look down and raise my eyebrows in shock when I see my fingers gripping his shaved head tightly. I have made sure that he stays right where he is. My body becomes lighter, yet my limbs feel heavy, and my pussy clenches tightly as pleasure builds deep inside me. Jeremiah grinds behind me, rubbing his erection up and down my ass crack.

"You like his hungry mouth against your pussy, don't you, Violet?" he groans, holding my ass cheeks together and sliding his cock between them. He's enjoying this as much as I am. Phoenix's tongue works faster, harder, all pointed right at my most sensitive area. My breathing grows heavy and fast. My cheeks flush and I cry out when the crest of my orgasm takes hold of my body. Shamelessly, I rock against Phoenix's face, while Jeremiah still rocks against my behind.

Phoenix pulls back, then slowly stands and swipes his damp lips with the back of his hand. "That was sweet," he drawls out.

"Too sweet, leader. I need something for me now," Jeremiah breathes over my shoulder. A new shudder runs over me as his hot breath brushes me. I'm still trying to catch my breath and get my head around the powerful eruption I have just released from my body.

My toes dip in my brother's cool blood that pools on the floor. I tentatively lift them, letting small droplets fall from my toes. My head lowers toward the ground, trying to avoid Phoenix's hungry gaze in front of me. I am more distracted with Jeremiah's blood ravenous glare at my back.

He instructs me again, his deep voice sounding over my shoulders. "Move your ass. I want you against the wooden pole."

Forgetting the blood on my feet, I plant my feet once more and walk to the center of the shed. I stand against the pole and begin to turn around but he grips my hips with force and growls.

"No, no, no! You don't face me, little flower," he snarls at me.

I focus back on the pole, my long hair tickling the curve in my back. Will I die now? Have I read this wrong? I don't feel like I have. And I am past the point of saving because I am not scared, but rather intrigued? No, that's not right. I am fucking starving for whatever this man is about to bestow upon me. I rub my trembling thighs together, the slick wetness coating the soft skin. My attention diverts to my red-stained hands. As they flutter over the rough wood, I swallow the big lump in my throat. My aging hands caused monstrous acts—they dismembered a body part less than an hour ago. But my pussy tells me it doesn't give a single fuck.

Hands rub against my bare ass, then slide up my back, landing heavily on my shoulders. I don't know whose hands they are. Rough callouses scrap my scarred skin, reminding me that in my thirty years I have also seen my share of lashings. I haven't always gotten away with having curious eyes. Sometimes simply breathing and being an outcast was enough.

Shadows dance around me as Jeremiah and Phoenix shift behind me, and the candlelight dances with them.

I hear the scraping of something and murmuring. I hold my breath, desperate to hear their words while sweat rolls down between my breasts.

Their murmuring stops as a figure walks around me. I watch the shadow on the dirt floor bobbing around as if water runs over it. I raise my head, meeting Jeremiah's intense stare. I wet my lips with my tongue when he holds barbed wire up in front of him. The corner of his mouth quivers and then morphs into a wicked smirk.

"Wrap your hands around the pole," he orders me.

I suck in a breath but comply. I link my fingers together in front of me, feeling my back arch. Phoenix's hands busy themselves, massaging my ass cheeks.

"You can't mean to use that to tie me up," I question him. He snorts and lays the first pieces of wire over my wrists.

"Oh I do mean to. You see..." he begins, lost in what I can only assume is his perfect world right now. He runs it under my wrist, causing me to hiss when I get pricked on the softer skin.

"I can make it just loose enough that it doesn't rip your skin apart while you are still, but it will be just tight enough that if you decide to move your hands and try to escape, it will tear your skin into pieces," he whispers.

He finishes looping it around my wrists, now binding me in my position against the wooden pole.

"Human bodies fascinate me. So sensitive. So easy to rip apart and kill. So easy to take away someone's last breath. So easy to get someone to the point of being able to hear their last heartbeat in their chest. But the human body can also be pleasurable. People think you need to be soft, sweet and gentle to feel that pleasure. But it can be laced with pain. They are the same thing," he tells me, his voice sounding far away.

I don't know if he is still here with us in the shed. His physical form is. But the rest of him I don't fucking know.

"Pleasure for you but pain for me?"

His eyes grow wide as he shakes his head from side to side. "You have it wrong. I will make you come harder than you have ever come before. I will make you scream my fucking name," he assures me.

Out of instinct, I try to back away, causing my wrists to pull against the wire. I pause quickly and hiss in pain. Tiny sharp holes develop around my wrists.

He clucks his tongue and laughs as he looks over my shoulder.

"You know sooner or later we have to kill her and that thing squirming behind us," Phoenix breathes against my neck as he rubs his erection up and down my ass crack.

"She will be our queen," Jeremiah answers him and drags a finger painfully slowly over my collarbone.

"I don't want to be queen of anything. I want to tear this place apart," I snarl, growing angry at that absurd suggestion.

"I will remind you that you said that."

Jeremiah moves out of my vision and I listen to him pick something off the work bench again. An instant later, something sharp runs over my bony spine. I arch my back and rattle my wrists.

"Don't move Violet, or your hands will end up falling from your arms while you watch." Jeremiah's voice caresses over me.

I bite the inside of my cheek and focus on keeping my arms as still as possible. Tiny red pinpoint-sized holes appear on my wrists as the barbed wire spikes rest heavily against them. A sharp yet slower scrape runs over my skin again but I fight my natural human reactions and hold still. I bear the sensation and close my eyes as I breathe out slowly. It's painful, but not unbearable. He runs the object over my skin again and this time I focus more on the sensation. It's not painful now. Was it not painful before?

The scrape runs down, stopping just above the top of my ass crack. I clench the muscles in the core of my vagina as tight as I can when a new feeling warms my body. The scraping turns erotic, tingling now, painful and scary.

I turn my head slightly, eyeing Phoenix, who is standing off to the side with his arms crossed over his chest. His focus is on what Jeremiah is doing to my back. While the pointed object is held firmly against my hip, fingers slip between my ass crack and rub it up and down. I lock eyes with Phoenix after he sucks in a breath and cranes his neck for a closer look. After staring me down for a moment, his attention slides back to what Jeremiah is doing to my behind. He rubs up and down against the opening, but never penetrates it. I couldn't help but arch my back and point my ass further back. Jeremiah's breathing grows heavy, quickening with every pass of my opening. His fingers move down further and rub into my pussy.

"You're dripping. Is that nice, Violet?"

"Yeah..." I breathe and lean my head against the wooden pillar. I'm not lying. This is erotic and fucking incredible. His fingers curve, pressing hard against the mound inside my pussy walls. I gasp at the beautiful pleasure and fist my hands tightly. My wrists move, causing the barbed wire to press deeper into my flesh. A whimper leaves my lips but it's not from the burning pain in front of me. It's from the intensifying pleasure that is behind me. Two thick fingers move inside of me, my wetness making it an easier task than it ever was with my brother. As his fingers move faster, slick sounds bounce off the shed walls. My breathing matches the savage speed, but it's not a speed I want to be slowed down.

I'm close to the edge that Phoenix got me to before, when Jeremiah abruptly stops. A throaty snarl tears from my throat and my eyes grow wide when I realize I sounded like a feral animal.

"That's right. Embrace your chaos, roll with the wild soul within you. You're broken like me. You are no better than us. You are us," he whispers against the side of my face, his breath pressing against my skin lightly. He rustles behind me before he grips one of my hips and presses his large tip at my opening.

I swallow thickly, about to argue with him and assure him that I am a lot better than him. But then I eye the blood on my fingertips again before I slowly drag my gaze down to my mangled breasts. Tears run down my cheeks when I realize his words are true. I am absolutely a monster. I dampen my lips with my tongue and close my eyes. Well, I guess only a monster will be capable of mass murder.

Jeremiah presses his tip further into me and groans. "Do you want all of it?"

"Yeah..." I purr out as the teasing becomes too much. The scraping starts on my back again...pressing harder this time. The pain is much worse than before.

"No, not that," I sob.

"Shhh, feel this for me, Violet..." he soothes me as he slowly fills my pussy with his hard cock. I moan loudly when the base of his cock meets my opening. "Focus on this..." He pulls his hips back and presses into me again. I arch my back further, creating friction against the mound inside my pussy.

He thrusts in and out at perfect speed and then he scrapes against my back again. The pain is too much and I no longer feel the pleasure.

My back feels wet, indicating to me that he has drawn blood.

"Violet, do you like my cock inside of you? I think you do because my cock is saturated with your desire," he says, distracting me from the pain.

Relentlessly, he thrusts deeper into me as he continues inflicting pain on my back. The pain is too much but so is the pleasure. My mind swims and I feel like I might finally pass out. Will the pain win or the pleasure?

Jeremiah reaches around and massages my clit, adding a new thick layer of pleasure. My legs grow weak and I moan against the wooden pole as it holds my weight.

"You are perfectly ripe for me. You bleed for me and drip juice all over my cock," he groans out. I pant loudly as he rolls his hips, coating his hips in my wetness.

"Clench your muscles," he instructs me. I know what muscles he means. I tighten my muscles and feel his thick, hard shaft even more, stretching me.

"Good girl," he croons and thrusts into me rapidly.

The pleasure builds quickly and it's so heightened that the pain on my back no longer seems relevant. I come brutally and smash my head against the wooden poll while Jeremiah fills me deeply with his seed as he cries loudly. Jeremiah runs his fingers over my back, slipping them through the fresh blood. It hurts. My back stings.

"What did you do to me?" I ask in a hushed voice.

He uses one hand to tuck himself away as he moves into my view. I gasp when I see the baseball bat in his other hand. Barbed wire wraps the thick end on it and is coated with my blood. The same bat I saw used the other night.

"Don't look at me like that. The cum on my cock tells me you didn't mind."

"I hate that bat!" I snarl.

Phoenix moves to the front of me and unwraps my wrists carefully with a deep frown across his forehead. "You didn't need to tear her skin apart like that," he tells Jeremiah.

Jeremiah shakes his head, holds up the bat and eyes the blood on it with a new cockiness. "Her back is a work of art. Now let's take care of that!" he growls deeply and points the bat at my brother.

CHAPTER 17

The three of us surround my bound brother. Gingerly, I huddle my coat around me. Although it stings my back and sticks to the blood, I am freezing.

The cold seeps into my bones, sending my body into a shivering frenzy. Am I in shock? A state of regret? Fear? Or simply just cold from being fucked naked in a shed? My thoughts spew through my brain while Jeremiah and Phoenix focus on my brother. Tears stream down his bright red cheeks. I snort sadly and close my eyes. I wonder if his tears are shock, fear or regret.

"What do we do with you? Outcast..." Phoenix asks quietly with a long sigh.

Jeremiah speaks up as he runs a hand roughly through his short hair. "He isn't worthy of being sacrificed in a fire to the gods."

Phoenix slides his eyes to Jeremiah with a confused frown creasing his forehead.

"What do you propose then? Can't hide the fucking severed cock, can we, so he can't be left to live amongst us!" Phoenix growls, looking at me so I know that his wrath doesn't bypass me. I twist my fingers in front of me as his glare makes me feel like he is threatening my life, not my brother's.

"I think he should go back to the ground. The ground can eat him, compost his rotting flesh and his bones will be lost forever along with his name and essence."

My attention is stolen by my brother who thrashes against his chair, shaking his head from side to side. There's no mistaking now—the emotion he feels is pure, cold fear. I nearly cave in. My human side that seems distant lately, tries to rear its emotional head, telling me this is horrible. *Wrong.* But I force my eyes to steel once more as I remember the angry snarls tearing from his throat while he raped me, time and time again.

"You are evil. Evil should be sent back to the grounds of hell," I whisper with agreement.

"It's settled. I shall grab a sack then," Phoenix says and turns toward a dark corner of the shed, where long sacks hang from a line of hooks. Phoenix brings them over as Jeremiah unfastens my brother and pulls him up into a standing position. My brother puts up a fight, not wanting to walk toward the sack that Phoenix dropped to the ground. Jeremiah's fist whips out and punches my brother in the kidney. My brother wheezes and lurches forward. Once Phoenix has finished spreading one of the bigger ones out, he stands back and waves his hands out with a smirk, gesturing him to get on it. I know my brother, though. He's a coward. Especially in the face of death.

My brother starts screeching against his tight gag and tries to back away with his chest giving loud panicked heaves.

Jeremiah kicks his leg out and hooks his booted foot around my brother's ankle, tripping him up. As he loses balance, Jeremiah forces him down onto the sack. Phoenix doesn't waste any time and drops to his knees and starts tying rope around his ankles while Jeremiah ties his hands against his stomach by putting rope around his torso. By the time they are finished, he looks like a wriggly worm.

Jeremiah ushers Phoenix off the sack and pulls one side over my brother and then reaches over him, clasping the other side in his fist. He smiles down at my brother as he slowly pulls the second side over him, covering his face and body completely now. Jeremiah looks to me and holds his hand out. "Pass me that rope behind you," he instructs me.

I look over my shoulder, the stretch hurting my back but I swallow my own pain down. I see the rope hanging over the chair he was on and grab it. After tossing it to Jeremiah, I watch him climb on top of my brother's heavily bound body and wrap the rope two times around him before tying a knot at the top. Still straddling him, he leans over his covered face and blows into it before chuckling under his breath. Slowly, he climbs off him and stands at the head while Phoenix moves around to his feet. "This is becoming the best night of my life, boss."

Phoenix scoffs and squats down, wrapping his arms around my brother's ankles and lifting.

"Tomorrow it's leader again to you...and to you." He looks over to me with a frown. "It's back to fucking silence otherwise it will be you in a sack," he finishes and sucks in a breath as my brother is lifted right off the ground now. "And grab a fucking shovel from beside the door," he orders me. I nod slightly and silently follow them outside, into the pitch black.

We make it through the sleeping village and stand at the start of the track that narrowly leads into the thick pine trees. I've never been this way before. It's out of bounds and to be fair, I have never had any desire to come down here.

They know the trail well and work their way quietly through the trees. Their heaving breathing and my brother's gagged cries are lost in the tall, thick forest. I take another step and trip, smashing my toes into what I can only assume is a tree root. The pain leaves a burning groan deep in my throat. I feel in front of me for Phoenix's back and cling to his shirt. He stops mid-step, tugging forward as Jeremiah tries to keep walking forward.

Phoenix grows so still as my hands desperately cling to him, in the hopes I won't get lost, or trip again.

"What the fuck is the problem?" Jeremiah hisses from the darkness.

"Argh, nah nothing. Keep going." The stutter gets lodged in his throat before Phoenix assures him and slowly continues walking. Should I apologize for needing him as my eyes right now?

Nah, fuck that.

A stronger wind picks up after another few minutes of walking. It's almost like a mixing bowl of wind coming from all directions. We must be out of the trees. My feet confirm this when my toes step on wet grass. Freshly settled frost is making the grass crispy and fucking painful. I may be cutting the tips of my toes off tonight when I get back if they are dead from frostbite.

It's a few more yards before we come to a halt. They place my wiggling brother on the ground and I drop the shovel by my feet. Only moonlight illuminates the clearing. But it's not a bright full moon so it doesn't help as much as I would like.

I hear rustling and look toward where I know Jeremiah is. A scratching sound follows before there's a tiny spark and flame. He lights a small candle from his pocket and places it on the ground by his feet.

"Welcome to the graveyard." He smiles at me and waves his arms around. Confusion is etched on my face as I stare back at him, but slowly, I cast my gaze around the dark clearing. I can't see anything at first. But not ten seconds later, my eyes begin to adjust and I make out objects. It's faint but when I squint and focus hard, I can definitely see them.

I take a few steps back and fall over, landing on my ass. I suck in a breath and feel around, my fingers meeting a mound of dirt. Vomit burns my throat and I scamper off it and back toward the shovel I just dropped. Swallowing thickly, I force the vomit down. I tripped on a grave. A fresh one by the feels. Rotting flesh is all around me.

Phoenix bends down and wraps his long fingers around the shovel and begins digging into the hard dirt. I sit on the ground, cold and wet but reluctant to move around a space I can't see clearly in.

Thud after thud echoes as the shovel makes contact with the earth. I don't know how much time passes but before long, Phoenix's puffed voice drifts down to me. "You going to bid farewell to your brother?"

I blanch and look up to his expectant gaze. "Seriously?"

"No I guess not." He chuckles and drops the shovel. Him and Jeremiah lift my brother once more and lay him down into the freshly dug grave. I wonder how they will kill him. Maybe strangle him. Would they let me do it? Could I?

I'm not left waiting for long. Jeremiah kneels beside me and pushes the shovel against my clasped hands. I look at him curiously. "What?"

"We dug the grave. You can fill it," he says.

"You going to kill him first?" I ask, rising to my feet and snatching the shovel from his hands.

"No...I don't think I will. Now begin," he instructs me.

"But if you're not going to kill him now and I bury him then..." I start.

Jeremiah cuts me off and snickers. "Ding ding, you get it. Now fucking begin," he growls after mocking me.

I don't trust these men, but I need them to complete a bigger goal. What's a saying I have heard from one of the males before? *I may lose the battle but I will win the war.* I get it now. And I don't trust that they won't quickly dig another grave for myself.

I begin to shovel up dirt and throw it down onto my brother. His body moves from side to side, but not far. I bury his feet first, slowly moving up his legs and torso. Sweat beads on my upper lip and my hands form blisters as I shovel in more soil. It's a while before the grave is completely full, aside from his head. His breathing is shallow. He can no longer move, but he still breathes. There is no mistaking it.

Slamming the shovel down into the dirt, I lift up another full scoop and hover it over his face. Tears spring to my eyes and I suck in my bottom lip. I am a monster. I am murdering a monster. I hold my breath and throw the dirt down onto his covered face. I hear one last muffled groan before I throw on another pile. A tear rolls down my cheek and drips down onto my mangled breast, now peeking through my open gown. Right at this moment, I feel like I am finally burying the last of my humanity and this is my own burial.

We leave the graveyard and head toward the village again. I still cling to Phoenix's back but this time traveling is faster and much easier. When we reach the entrance of the village, Jeremiah swerves off toward where I know his own cabin resides. He seems cold again. Hateful, actually. Like the past two hours together never happened.

"Come," Phoenix says and pulls me in the other direction toward my own cabin. He pushes open my old, rusty door and closes it behind us. My candles are dim but they still burn enough.

"I will make sure someone brings you a pail of water to bathe tomorrow." He leans his back against my door. I nod once and look at my small cot. I am really exhausted now the night is coming to an end.

"Why do you insist on this life? Why do I have to pretend tonight never happened tomorrow and I don't know my own voice?"

"Because in this life you need to be powerful. I need power over you and everyone else. And this life? This life isn't so fucking bad. At least we have order and a functioning village here. Out there...It's not as good as you may think."

"Why the obsession with power?" I sniff and sink down onto my bed.

"Oh naive Violet. Because power is safety in this world. Without power we are vulnerable, ready for the vultures to pick apart."

I say nothing. I don't want his words to make sense. I climb under my blanket and pull it high above me so it nestles against my chin.

Floorboards creak as Phoenix pushes off the door and moves toward me. He sinks down beside my legs, his warmth giving me more comfort than it should.

"I can show you what power can give you. Name something you want."

"Anything?"

"Anything but your freedom..." he answers honestly. Candlelight flickers against his straight jaw, dancing over his short stubble.

"I want shoes and a warmer blanket," I reply after a thought.

His hands move under my blanket, finding my feet. As his warm fingers wrap around my freezing toes, he dips his chin. He rubs my feet a few times before standing up.

"I will see what I can do. Make sure you put an antiseptic on your back. That barbed wire isn't exactly clean." He heads to the door and pauses in the open doorway. "Also if you think you don't hold any power in this cult, then you are very wrong. You hold way too much power over me and have for a very long time."

The door shuts and I pull the blanket over my head, creating a warm cocoon. My breath warms the space around me and I close my eyes. But all I am met with is the reminder of my brother bound in a sack in the cold dark earth. I rip the blanket off my head as a shiver runs through my body. I will deal with freezing.

CHAPTER 18

T he next morning my whole body aches. The sky outside is still moody, murky with the remains of the stars and dark night. I must have only slept for a couple of hours, but I'm surprised I slept at all.

Gingerly, I get dressed in my appropriate full gowns. When I was told business as usual, I tend to believe them. But as I slip my last arm into my long gown sleeve, I wince at the burning pain in my back and let out a big sigh at the gruesome reminder of what I did last night.

Have I become the villain in my own story? The scariest thing is I don't think I really care...it is more just an observation. While I stretch my ankles, rolling them from side to side, I note that I will be chained soon. I slowly cast a glance over the subtle scratched marks on the cabin floor. The chain rubbing against the floorboards every day for the last twenty-odd years has left almost a faint Y shape. It shows the once tedious, then soon-to-become comfortable routine I have had every day. A line from my work bench to the shelves of ingredients and oils, then to my personal space where my cot is.

Shuffling slowly, I make my way to the shelves and snag my dried turmeric powder and some ginger root. I move to my work bench and pull out the small metal frame I had made for myself many years ago. In the center of it is a small circular hole, the right size for some candles to be placed. I put two candles in the center, lighting them with my flint and placing a small saucepan over the top. I then pour in a little water, turmeric powder and a chunk of ginger. This is going to be a slow process. It always is when I heat up teas and water or make oils. But this is what I have. It's not like I don't have endless time to stand here anyhow. I watch over the liquid concoction in front of me and decide to sprinkle in some more turmeric. It's a lot stronger than I would normally allow but I know my body needs all the help it can get.

Soon, the mixture in front of me should become a heated shot of pain relief. Jeremiah and Phoenix weren't kind enough to leave me some. I drum my nails on the work bench and look out to the sky that still shows the remnants of night with a frown creasing my forehead.

Last night I felt pleasure that I never knew possible. They didn't compete with each other—they worked in sync, getting pleasure from controlling me simultaneously. Those men that always scared me, made my skin crawl and made me want to shrink away to the size of a dust particle, have all of a sudden shifted in my own eyes. I am no longer scared of them in a sense of dreading death. I look at them now and find them more curious.

I curl my toes on the cold floor, remembering Phoenix's soft touch on them last night. I try to pinpoint exactly when my feelings for him really shifted. The mating ceremony when he stared into my soul with his hard cock? Or the day in the herb garden when he scorned me, but also didn't beat me for breaking every rule we have. I can't pinpoint anything. Things have shifted, changed. Maybe it's purely down to the fact I no longer care about death, because after my nipples, pain no longer bothers me. I have realized pain can be a state of mind. Despite all the events and pondering thoughts, it remains. Phoenix can show kindness in his own way. Jeremiah still feels like the grim reaper to me, but he holds a power that I seem to be drawn to. The monster in me claws at the surface, wanting to be let out when he is around. Instead of me hiding the fact I want to torture and kill everyone, whenever he is around, I want to skip around him and tell him every dark thought, knowing full well he will clap and cheer and then fucking join in.

They are polar opposites, yet a steady tingle starts between my legs when I think of the gentle touch of Phoenix's fingers on my pussy and the brutal pain of Jeremiah at my back. I wonder if I can handle them both at the same time.

I blow a steadying breath out through my pursed lips as my cheeks flush at the erotic thought. I think I may really like that.

I hear the clatter of bulky keys before the thud sounds out when the key is shoved into my rusty door lock. I slowly shake my head from side to side and take another long breath as I desperately try to force the sexual tension from my body and mind.

The door creaks loudly as it opens, a gust of wind following it. I scrunch my eyes as I try to listen more closely. I hear more than one lot of footsteps. Slowly, I turn around to see who is in my cabin. Phoenix stands in the doorway with a small girl who's holding a pail of steaming water.

Her hair is blonde and long enough to reach her shoulders. At least, long for the age I assume her to be. She looks to be no older than five. Her face is pointed down toward the ground, hands firmly around the pail handle and shoulders inwardly slumped.

I step backward, my hips hitting the edge of my work bench. Goose-bumps erupt over my arms as a chill settles in my bones. I look at her and see myself, in my old cult. I used to do chores like this when I wasn't serving my father and brother. I used to take food and water to prisoners. Slowly, I raise my eyes to Phoenix and let out a long sigh. He doesn't know about my old life. He isn't to blame but I still fucking hate him right now.

His eyes roam my face then dangerously slow down my body. Eventually, they creep back up to my face and his eyebrows settle low over his eyes.

"Serenity is here with your water to bathe. You can also use the warm water to make your oats. She is in training. Should she make eye contact, speak or anything out of the cult ways, I know you will indicate to us that she has broken the law so she can be punished appropriately."

I scrunch my nose up at his words and look toward the little girl once more. I see a shiver run over her entire body. Or is that my imagination? Maybe she feels and thinks nothing. Or maybe...just maybe...she has a loud brain like I did at her age.

"You getting sick?" Phoenix's voice shatters my deep thoughts.

I look back at him. He rests a shoulder against the door frame, thick wool coat hanging from his board shoulders. He runs a hand over his prickly head as he raises an eyebrow at me.

Finally, I remember my erotic thoughts from earlier and the remains of my flushed cheeks that I am sure are still evident.

I part my lips to answer him but he clears his throat just in time to catch my thoughtless act. I side eye the girl and dip my head, turning it from side to side slowly to give him an answer.

After a brief moment, I look at him and see the start of a smirk tug at the corner of his lips.

"Catch you in a *bad* moment?" His eyes dip to my crotch and then back to my face where he bites his bottom lip. It pisses me off. Fuck him for knowing exactly what my body was wanting.

I shake my head but don't drop the eye contact. He scowls and clears his throat.

"Let's be a good example for young Serenity here, shall we? Would hate to see you both flogged side by side," he growls and diverts his attention. "Place the water on the ground and head back to your quarters. Morning chores are to be completed."

Serenity follows his orders and places it on the ground then backs away, her feet slowly sliding along the ground until she is met with the cold, open door again. She turns and steps out from my cabin. Phoenix pushes off the door frame and moves toward me. So slowly, like he is making his steps careful and measured so he doesn't fuck up our cover either.

He gets to me, places a hand lightly on my hip and glides it down as he sinks to his knees. His hand grazes my knee as he finds the hem of my gown and moves his hand up my bare leg. His hand runs up my calf muscle and rests just below my knee. I lift my leg out slightly so my foot is just off the ground. Like an animal in the wild, Phoenix rubs his jaw stubble against the sensitive skin on my leg before slowly dragging a tongue over my calf where his hand just was. His shoulders vibrate as a quiver runs over his back.

He coughs quietly and moves his hand back down to my ankle, where he uses his other hand to secure the shackle around it. He locks it into place before he slowly stands.

"How's your back?" he asks me, his breath against my face.

"Why are you being nice to me all of a sudden?"

"I could have had you ripped from naval to throat." He runs a lone finger over me to emphasize where he means. "For all that talking you do," he says quietly as he runs that same finger over my mouth. "I have kept you alive for a long time, Violet. I have always been nice to you. Your existence takes up the majority of my thoughts every day."

"So me being vocal and breaking every law we have gives you a hard cock and you like the feeling?" I ask sarcastically and roll my eyes. I really can't help it. Honestly.

His hand brushes over my breasts and his fingers find the soft skin on the side of my head.

"I do indeed enjoy my hard cock," he drawls. Then stares me straight in the eye with his eyebrows pulled heavily over them in a frown. "But my position in this village is my priority. Don't ever forget that. I would like to have both, but if that doesn't seem possible, I will make an executive decision that looks after my interests alone," he finishes and brings his lips closer to my face. His lips against my own lightly before he pulls back.

"Have a lovely day Violet," he says as he walks out of my cabin.

CHAPTER 19

Wake up. Shackled. Eat. Create. Eat. Sleep.

It goes on and on for days. The winter season has just begun, yet there's already an instant change in the wind. It's colder, crisper and drying on the skin and lips, yet full of moisture. Winter never really makes sense. Though some of our berries seem to yield larger crops when we get more frosts. I am sure there are more positives, but to me, that seems to be the only thing that makes sense in winter.

I scrape my finger across the fresh condensation on the window glass and watch the disrupted water droplets roll down to the sill.

The door rattles and I turn to wait to see who it is. Eenie meenie...

Jeremiah's fingers grip the handle hard as he pushes it open fully. His inhuman eyes find me in an instant. I drop my shoulders and divert my gaze down toward the ground.

"The women are here to grab satchels of winter tea," he grunts, blending himself into the corner of my cabin as three women walk in. I can see their damp boots pace across the floor with my lowered view. Frowning, I keep my head down. They shouldn't all need more winter tea yet. I clear my throat and don't move.

"Problem, slave?" Jeremiah calls out. This means I can answer since he asked me a question.

"I—I need time to make some more up. They have gone through it faster than expected."

"Yes, because you fucked up, Violet. You only gave them all half portions. Your mind must have been on something else. Maybe I should beat you in front of everyone."

Now I know something is up, because I would never risk my own hide by giving them all the incorrect amounts.

"My mistake. Please forgive me and my pathetic female brain. I will make some more as fast as possible."

It's faint but I swear I can hear Jeremiah cough and chuckle when I call myself a pathetic female. It takes everything in me not to glare at him and spit some colorful cuss words.

"Well, I suppose I can't expect much more from a reject and the lesser human gender in our world," Jeremiah says in a mocking tone. *He's trying to bait me.* Does he want to beat me in front of everyone?

I bite down on the inside of my cheek and refuse to give in to him. Giving myself a moment to breathe, I answer slowly. "Maybe you have some jobs to do while I make the satchels. I would hate for you to get bored," I suggest, hoping he will get lost.

The air in the room changes and becomes so thick with tension that I almost choke on it. A girl in front of me moves a foot slightly, which is all I have to know that they all feel uncomfortable and probably scared right now.

Jeremiah's boots thud across the flooring and he reaches me in just a few mere steps. He grips my hair hard and pulls my head back savagely so my back is arched. It hurts so bad, with the fresh scabs breaking open. A quiet whimper escapes my lips. But he doesn't care. He headbutts me and spits down on the side of my jaw. It dribbles down then drops off onto my covered shoulder.

"Never suggest anything to me again. You answer if we fucking ask, otherwise shut your mouth, dog," he growls then quietly adds in my ear, "Unless I ask you to open your mouth."

My head swims with dizziness from the headbutt so I consider the fact I may have dreamed that. He lets go of my hair and faces the other women.

"I need to gather our border patrol. As soon as she is done, head back and start your chores."

Feeling blood trickle down my temple, I wipe my sleeve over my damp jaw. I've lost all my patience now and raise my head to look at the women. I've seen all three of them around the village. The one in the middle is the one I saw getting her ass carved with barbed wire on a bat. The one who also got mated recently.

I cross my arms over my chest, ignoring the fresh blood on my head and back, with my mousey brown hair now sitting messily over one shoulder.

"I'm not stupid. What the fuck is going on?" I have never been this thoughtless before. But their conniving lies could have cost me my life.

The three females in front of me keep their demeanor unchanged. Their shoulders are low, their heads even lower, breathing even and hands relaxed behind their backs. Picture perfect. That same foot moves again. I let out a long sigh and swipe the wet blood on my head with the back of my hand. Rolling my hand from side to side, I inspect the blood before shaking my hand, sending droplets across the front of my skirt.

"Tell me what you need. If you don't talk now, you won't get the chance."

Their heads turn to one another, side eyeing each other.

The middle one, named Aurelia from memory, looks to me for the first time. Her eyes twitch before she glances around the room, bouncing off every surface.

She's nervous.

"Time's ticking..." I say quietly. I want to help these women. That was my original goal. But even I am getting impatient.

Aurelia's mouth opens and her eyes widen. But she's still not saying anything.

"Do you know how to speak?" I ask again, quietly trying to keep her as calm as possible.

She shakes her head from side to side. She coughs and points to her tummy. I frown, watching her movements closely.

"You need medicine for a sore tummy?" I ask slowly. Poor bitch is probably already pregnant. That's always the goal here, I suppose.

But she shakes her head to me again and frantically points to her stomach. My frown deepens with only more confusion setting in.

"Pain? Nausea?" I question her. Her head shakes wildly with tears springing to the corners of her eyes. I look toward the woman on her left and raise a confused eyebrow at her.

She glances over the blood on my forehead, like it's a threat to her own life. I guess it's a small reminder of this exchange we are having now. Even them looking at me is cause for concern over all our lives. Slowly, she lifts her arms and brings them together in front of her. With her forearms overlapping, she rocks her arms from side to side. Realization dawns on me as I flick my attention back to Aurelia.

"You're with child?" I ask. She nods her answer to me and swipes at a rogue tear.

"So what do you want? Vitamins? Nausea tea? Everything you could want is what the doctor can give you," I assure her.

She shakes her head and opens her mouth again "Don—t," she stutters and spits the 'T' sound out. She knows how the word should sound but she doesn't know how to make it.

I remember women in my old cult would talk in hushed voices if they really needed to. They thought they were stealthy, but even I would hear them sometimes. Here, the women are so scared they don't even dare consider learning to talk.

I have seen the odd toddler with a sewn mouth if they were loud and tried to speak. It breaks my heart.

"Don't what?" I ask and look between all of them. The one to the left raises her hands again but runs a thumb across her throat this time.

"You don't want the baby?" I ask skeptically.

She nods as a shiver runs through her.

"Oh hell no. You realize what that will mean for you if they found out?"

She cries and pushes her hands together in a praying fashion. "Please?"

"How do you know I can even give you something to kill the fetus?"

She chews her lower lip and stares at me.

My reputation preserves me clearly. Also, maybe I am not as careful as I think.

"Tell me honestly—are you prepared for the fact that if you do this, we may all die?" I ask because I am ready for death if it comes to that but I don't think they really are.

"I'd rather die than watch more babies mutilated at their hands," the woman on the right bursts out. I gawk at her and for the first time in a while, I am shocked to the point of speechlessness and thoughts no longer manifest.

Finally, I breathe out, "You can talk? Very well too…"

"My first baby was a boy. Treated like a god. It's how I thought it should be. My daughter was born and got her lips sewn shut when she was four years old. It didn't feel right any longer. If it was right, why did my heart scream in pain for her? I have taught myself to talk ever since then. I need to be my daughter's voice too."

"What's your name?" I ask. The other two shake in what I can only assume is a new fear. Things have just changed. A lot.

"Skye," she says and I nearly cry. I'm proud of her. She raises her chin slightly and squares her shoulders.

"I will put something together for you, Aurelia. You will need to drink it in one go. It is not promised to work, but if it does, be prepared for a lot of pain and mess."

I turn and drag my chain across toward the shelves of herbs and spices. I reach up to the very top shelf. It's the same shelf I often glance at in desire to inflict pain, but never use.

Plucking off three jars, I return to my work bench where I mix small amounts of each in a small glass of cold water. It would be more ideal and probably nicer in warm water, but it doesn't really matter. The only thing that matters is that she ingests all three ingredients.

I pass it to her and she tips her head back, drinking it all down without hesitation. She hands the empty glass back to me and nods in a thank you gesture.

"You guys better leave. You have already been here for too long," I say and they all turn to leave.

"Wait!" I gasp, nearly forgetting something. I reach under my work bench and pull out some satchels of winter tonic that I always keep in abundance. I hand them all a satchel as a cover.

They take it from me and leave. Skye pauses in the door frame and looks back at me. "I would say, talk soon as the men say, but I don't think we will."

"No, I suppose you are right."

Chapter 20

Night time comes. Wind howls outside. The windows rattle as I sit on the edge of my cot, watching the glass shake against the strain. I hug myself tightly with a frown creasing my forehead. I wonder if we are getting our first big winter storm. A cyclone always tests the strength of our cabins and our winter supplies because it will normally flatten the winter veggie garden.

Normally I can smell the rain in the air but when the wind starts first, it's anyone's guess.

My door bangs, with someone trying to enter. *It's not locked,* I think to myself as I glance at my shackled ankle.

The wind forces it to fly open and I see Phoenix standing there with his arms full. He paces inside and hooks his booted foot around the door and kicks it shut. With a huff, he drops the contents in his arms onto the foot of my bed. I look over them curiously and run my fingers through the rabbit fur before lifting it up. Underneath there is a thick layer of wool, knitted into a blanket lining. The older ladies in the village are tasked with making all the linen and clothing. They have done a nice job on this. I unravel it, seeing it's the perfect sized blanket for my bed. A hand around my shin steals my attention and I look down to see Phoenix's hand gripping it intensely.

He sucks in a breath as he unlocks my shackle and throws it across the ground.

It lands against the foot of my work bench in a loud heap. His head doesn't stray from my direction though. His heated eyes burn into me.

"You finally got me a blanket?" I ask in a hungry whisper.

The corners of his lips dance with a smirk and he rises up on his knees before planting both his hands on my thighs.

"I am here to serve dear Violet," he breathes and begins lifting my gown.

"I have never had a slave before." My dry humor is returned with a mischievous grin from Phoenix.

"Tell me what you want? What do you want me to do?"

"Why?" I wonder if this is a trick.

"I tell people what to do all day. Tell me, Violet, how do you want me to look after you right now?" he asks just as the rest of my gown is bunched at my hips, revealing my pussy that is only hidden by a small, thin layer of cotton.

His breath flows hot against the inside of my thigh. I tense at the warm flicker that brushes against my panties, drawing heat like a magnet.

"I want your hot tongue to warm my pussy," I say on a breath.

Without hesitation, his finger hooks in the crotch of my panties and he shifts them to the side. His lips brush against the outside of my pussy, planting soft sweet kisses over it. I look down, watching Phoenix adore what I have to offer. Wanting to satisfy me is satisfying him. I feel powerful.

I clench my muscles and run a hand over his prickly scalp before I grip the back and hold his head in place. He doesn't get mad. He becomes enthralled even more. I watch him close his eyes in delight and part his mouth. Tilting his head just slightly, he slides out his tongue and flicks it over my desperate clit. I buck slightly at the intense pleasure that comes with the new movement. But he doesn't stop. It only encourages him more. I moan when his tongue finds my clit again and it seems to please him. His fingertips grip my thighs and he pulls my crotch to him more. He lingers, savoring every moment. But I prefer what he did before.

"Go back to my clit," I whisper in desperate desire.

He whimpers quietly, like he is disappointed I am taking it away from him. My skin is ablaze with desperate need. Being powerful adds to the level of sensation.

"I said I want you back to satisfying my clit," I bite out through clenched teeth. My cheeks flush as he reluctantly slides his tongue back up and swirls it over my clit.

"Yeah like that!" I gasp and hold his head like a primal animal. He has me suspended on the edge of being utterly undone and an unbearable need.

He moves his tongue faster, causing the pleasure in me to build. My skin feels hot, leaving a sheen of sweat all over my body. Breathing heavily, I lean my head back and let myself be lost to the erotic pleasure. It feels like it is too much, like I can't take any more or I might die. But I do take more. Greedily, I take everything Phoenix's delicious tongue has to give me. I moan loudly and my thighs shake against either side of his head. His tongue swirls around and the tip of it flicks over my sensitive clit. I gasp and cry out as the crest of my orgasm hits me hard. Quickly, I grip his head and hold onto it for dear life, keeping it completely still as my entire pussy becomes too sensitive.

I feel like I am burning from the inside out, but the feeling is one I want to last forever.

Slowly as the feeling resides, I shuffle away from Phoenix and lie back on my bed. My heavy breathing fills my cold cabin, with the clouds of steam swirling above me. Phoenix rises up and leans over me. His eyes look concerned. I raise an eyebrow at him.

"Can I feel you now?" he asks. No, it's more like begging.

"Feel what?" I ask, confused.

"You. Can I feel your pleasure on my starved cock? *Please?*"

I look down between my legs and his head dips, following my line of sight.

"I guess you have earned that," I say, giving him permission which still doesn't feel right.

He lifts himself onto my small bed, which feels even smaller now with him on it. He climbs between my legs and pulls my new blanket over his body, covering us both. I freeze when he inserts a large finger into my pussy and twirls it around. But not long after he removes it, I hear him sucking on his finger. His eyes drift shut, with a fresh flush coloring his cheeks.

"So, so good," he drawls.

He nudges my legs wider apart with his hips as his hard cock presses against my opening. He is big, but I know what it feels like now to be wet and ready. His hips move forward slightly so the tip makes its entrance. I feel full already. I arch my back and lean my head back. He buries his head in my curtain of hair while he struggles for control.

"Take a deep breath, Violet," he whispers against my head.

I suck in a breath and as I do, he inches in more. I move my legs apart further, trying to help but I already feel so full. I grip his back, my nails finding all his straining muscles.

"It's okay, breathe out now," he placates me.

I listen to him and breathe out slowly. He pushes the rest of his big cock in until the base is flush against my pussy. This feels so intimate. His hard body over mine is warm. For the first time ever, I feel vulnerable in a new sense. I need to remind myself I am using these men to achieve my own goal. But I feel so comforted right now, and gloriously warm.

He pulls his hips back before slowly gliding forward again. "Perfect. It feels better than I have ever imagined and I have imagined a lot."

He continues moving inside me, taking his time and reassuring me. I suck in my bottom lip and moan when he moves a hand under my backside and lifts it slightly. He picks up his pace while holding that position, finding a new g-spot deep within me that I didn't know I had.

"Are you okay?" he asks me.

"Yeah," I moan into his shoulder, holding him as close to me as possible.

"You bring me to my knees, Violet. Always have and always will," he groans and thrusts painfully deep. He cries out as his hot cum spasms deep inside of me, his body rocking with pleasure. Slowly, he draws out of me just slightly, but his cock is still hard. My brother always went soft straight after. My eyes flutter. I feel exhausted but I don't want him to move. He is warm and it's something I've never had before.

"Go to sleep, dear Violet. Let me enjoy this while you rest," he orders me, pushing back into me again. He doesn't want it to end. Neither do I but it doesn't take much persuasion. My eyes flutter briefly before I close them and succumb to the first warm sleep I have had in a very long time.

I wake to a thud and then a snarl that could belong to an animal. I try to turn over in bed and look at who or what is entering my cabin but my legs are stuck in place. Phoenix's warm and very asleep body is still nestled between my legs.

"This is a whole 'nother level of weird," I whisper under my breath.

The blanket is ripped off me, but before I can scream, a hand is flattened over my mouth. Stubble rubs up and down my jawline before Jeremiah's voice envelopes my hearing. "Phoenix is losing the fucking plot and you're not helping," he growls.

"Phoenix can fucking hear you. Shouldn't you be in your sleeping quarters?" Phoenix growls back.

"I saw you come in here hours ago and never left. You think other people won't notice," Jeremiah bites out in frustration. I can do nothing but lie there in muffled silence.

Phoenix climbs out from between my legs, leaving a cold airy space where he just was.

"Don't ever question my actions. I have been the leader for a long time and plan to keep being the leader."

"Maybe my faith in that is a little blurred right now," Jeremiah admits bravely. I shudder under him. Phoenix has been different but I have also spent twenty years watching his brutality toward anyone that disrespects him.

"Hmm, if that is what you need to think."

Jeremiah doesn't move. He does remove his hand a little, slipping it down to my throat where he rubs his thumb backward and forward slowly on the sensitive part of the skin.

"You shouldn't say things like that to Phoenix. I have seen what he is capable of."

"No, I think I should say things like that to him. He needs motivation to prove to everyone why they should respect him."

Phoenix scoffs at the remark and stands close to the door.

"Maybe him being nice isn't a bad thing. I like him being nice to me," I admit before I realize how insane that sounds about the man that has terrified me most my life.

He snickers, irritating me. I tense under his weight and spit into his face.

His hand wraps around my neck roughly and he drags me from my bed. I wheeze, beating at his hands, but he pulls me up and slams me against the wall, never releasing his grip.

"Lick it off," he barks into my face.

"No," I gasp, needing him to loosen his grip. That is feral, but I shouldn't be surprised. What does surprise me is that being a victim of his merciless hands can leave me wet between my thighs. The sting his hand inflicts on me somehow begins to feel like home. There is a dangerous longing developing within myself that feels like this is what I need.

"I said, lick it off," he says slowly again and lets my neck go a little.

I don't want to obey him. I liked feeling powerful with Phoenix, but my body tells me it does want to obey. My body tells me that it would feel natural to walk into a burning building with this man.

I part my lips and swipe my tongue against the now cool saliva splattered over his cheek.

"Now spread your legs for me," he orders me. I spread them and hook one leg onto his hip. He reaches between us and pulls his hard cock free. The tip rubs against my opening as he rocks his hips backward and forward.

"Open your mouth," he says.

I listen to him, opening my mouth and waiting for what he wants me to do next. I grow wetter with each second that passes.

His head hovers just above mine and he looks down at me, pursing his lips. He sucks in a long breath and spits down into my open mouth.

"Shut your mouth and swallow it."

I should be gagging; I should be dry retching and running. But instead, I close my mouth and swallow his warm saliva.

"Good girl Violet," Jeremiah praises me as he thrusts into me. A fiery inferno erupts through me as soon as he shows me how much I have pleased him. A quiver starts in my thighs, becoming weak as the need grows.

He groans when he is deep, his pelvis pressed tightly against my own. He lifts my leg high and pulls me with him as he steps away from the wall.

"You going to stand there, or you going to help me fill our naughty Violet?" Jeremiah speaks over his shoulder while his hips pull back, dragging his big cock slowly out of my pussy. Just as the tip rests in my opening, he thrusts it back in, sliding the length against my g-spot. I close my eyes and lean my head back as I struggle not to combust. Warmth meets me in a hard, muscled frame. My head nestles back against Phoenix's shoulder and in one hungry motion his arm wraps around my hips. He clings to me while he rubs my ass cheeks with his erection. No words or sounds come from him, but his quick breathing brushes over my shoulder and down my breasts.

Phoenix reaches down as Jeremiah glides out of me again and grips his cock. My eyelids flutter open. I look down my naked body and watch Phoenix fist Jeremiah's cock. His knuckles turn white as he tugs his hand up and down it with strength.

Jeremiah groans into my face before his teeth cling to his lower lip. I want to come right here, yet neither of them are physically pleasuring me right now. Phoenix slides his hand over the cock a few more times before he clutches my pussy and coats his hand in my wetness. His hand snakes behind me where he rubs my ass with his slippery hand. Jeremiah greedily pushes back into me with his hand still gripping one thigh nice and high. He inserts a finger into my ass and I gasp at the unnatural intrusion. It's not painful but rather uncomfortable.

"Shh, relax Violet." Phoenix whispers into my hair while he slides his finger out and back in. I take a deep breath and grip Jeremiah's shoulders. He pulls his hips back and rubs his hand over my pussy then reaches past me and lubricates Phoenix's cock. He nods once and then starts fucking me again with a slightly faster rhythm. Phoenix spreads my ass cheeks and rubs his slick tip over my opening, teasing me. It's undeniable what his intentions are and the anticipation grows but with every thrust from Jeremiah against my stretched pussy, it's just enough to keep me in a state of desirable hunger. Phoenix presses the head in and quickly grips my hips as my entire body shudders. His knees bend slightly while he perfects his position for penetration. He stays still for a moment, allowing me some time to adjust. After a moment he then pushes forward. My ass stretches painfully, a hot stinging erupting with every movement he makes.

He groans loudly once his hips are flush against my ass cheeks.

"She taking all of you?" Jeremiah asks between panted breaths. He moves in and out of me fast, while his balls slap loudly against me.

"Of course," Phoenix drawls and slides out of me. He is slower, careful.

"Of course she is. You're our good girl aren't you Violet?"

I pinch his shoulders harder as Phoenix's cock slides back in again.

"Say it. Say you are our good girl." Jeremiah says and leans his sweaty forehead against my own.

"I am your good girl." I reply, but it comes out in a beg. The stinging is beginning to turn to pleasure and the fullness in me doesn't appease my hunger for them.

"Yeah you are." Phoenix bites out and moves faster now. My legs no longer hold me up but they both do. The slapping of bodies intertwines with the heavy breathing.

I drop one hand and slide my hand down my stomach, seeking my swollen clit. I rub two fingers over it and cry loudly when my body erupts in a thunderous release.

"Fuck!" Jeremiah yells and presses against me hard as he fills me with his cum. His cock spasms inside of me and I cling to his shoulders.. Phoenix slams hard against my ass, stretching me so much I can feel every vein and spasm deep inside me.

They both pull out of me, leaving me feeling empty and cold. Phoenix walks around me and heads back toward the door, but he pauses and raises his eyes to meet mine. His flushed cheeks tighten when a satisfied smirk tugs at his mouth. He pulls the door open and disappears.

"You may like your nice leader because he gives you little comforts, but when you feel like going on a killing spree again and letting your alter ego out, I know exactly whom you will seek out. And it won't be him," he says in a stern rush before he leaves, finally slamming my cabin door behind him.

I hug myself and sink back down into my bed, tucking myself into my new winter weight blanket.

I stare into the darkness, sleep now alluding to me. He is right and that pisses me off more than I care to admit.

CHAPTER 21

I am a monster. I know that. But as I clean my inner thighs with a damp cloth, I consider the fact we are all monsters. What is right and what is wrong? Maybe there isn't right or wrong—maybe there is just living until we live no longer.

Is Aurelia a monster for aborting her baby? Is Phoenix a monster for running a village full of heathens? Am I a monster for enabling the abortion and killing my own brother?

Or is Aurelia simply saving a baby from a life of hell, so she is doing a kindness? Is Phoenix simply running a village the only way he has been shown how, the only life he has ever lived so he is simply ignorant and carrying childhood trauma? Am I simply a victim that took care of a predator so he could no longer hurt anyone ever again?

I drop the cloth into the metal pail and push it to the side before I stand and take my clean gown off. I grunt and twist my long hair into a messy bun, securing it with a stick from dried rosemary.

Looking out my small window, I watch the women gather ripe foods from the garden in preparation for the day's meals. Curiously, I watch them all a little differently today. I thought they were all completely under the spell of the magicians of evil. But after reflecting on last night, I now ponder who talks in secret, who steals a glance when they think no one is looking. And who has a repulsion to the life they endure every day.

Jeremiah and a few guards march through the center of the vegetable garden, not giving a shit what they trample. Jeremiah stops short and leans his head into a few other guards that meet them in the middle, where they seem to be talking seriously.

So much is happening in this freaky town, I deliriously chuckle to myself. Jeremiah twirls his index finger around, signaling the men to group up and he paces off. His head swivels in my lone cabin's direction and he glares through the window. We lock eyes, just briefly, then—as if nothing happened, he turns his head forward again and keeps marching with five men following close behind, their rifles strapped to their backs.

There is movement outside my door and I glance at my ankle that I know will be shackled in a moment. Phoenix walks in, a fiery look in his face with eyes that could cut someone in half like a sharp knife.

I cross my arms over my chest and lean against my work bench, feeling a little at ease with Phoenix here. Not a feeling I wanted to feel at all but right now I don't fight against it. They were meant to be my stepping stones in a game of retribution. I settle my eyes on him, knowing he won't really hurt me.

"I need you on breakfast duty this week."

I frown at him and drop my arms to my sides. "Why? I like being hidden in here away from you freaks..." I grind out but it comes off a little playful.

"We have one of the females with the doctor. Seems like she is losing her baby but there are complications," he says sternly without taking those lethal eyes away from my face.

"Wh-what complications?"

"She's losing too much blood. Anyhow you can help with food."

"Will she be okay?"

His eyelids lower slightly as he hones his attention. He looks over me more critically, leaving me feeling exposed. "Why the fuck do you care? You never care."

I swallow and push off the edge of the work bench, standing straight. "You are right. I don't care. I will help with food. Hopefully I won't add poison to it."

"I would take you seriously but I know you wouldn't cross the line of killing young children, would you?" he says but it comes across as an open enquiry.

I lick my lips, trying to rid them of the anxious dryness and walk toward Phoenix. He grips my upper arm and stops me abruptly before I can walk through the door. "It's not lost on me that she was one of the women that came to you."

As soon as he lets me go, I lurch forward and stumble out of the threshold and walk toward the community hall. I have never helped with food preparation before. I have eaten here on rare days but aside from that, I'm either brought food or I eat whatever broth I can create.

While I keep my eyes low, I grip either side of my dress. My hands should be behind me, clasped at my back, but the perspiration on my fingers steals my thoughts.

Raising my leg, I step up onto the porch that wraps around the front of the building. The wood shudders and creaks under me but I ignore it and keep moving forward. The simple door is already ajar and I press my fingertips against the cool wood. Looking over my shoulder briefly, I find Phoenix busy in conversation with some other men. I lick my lips and push the door open and walk in. Creeping around, I see a square archway that leads to what only sounds like cooking. I follow the noise of banging pots and pans and enter a space I have never been allowed before.

There is a smell of boiling vegetables and hot animal fat. Glancing around, I notice the long cast iron cooktop and underneath it is a long narrow fireplace with smoldering embers. No one looks at me, or even flinches when I enter. Well trained and well scared.

An elderly woman places a sack on the table beside me and tosses a small sharp knife beside the sack. The knife clatters as it settles onto the smooth wood. Lifting my hand, I push the opening of the sack so I can see what it holds. There are large potatoes covered in a dusting of soil. I sigh and wrap my fingers around the hilt on the knife before picking up a potato and begin peeling.

The women around me work cohesively and without a single word. I hate this feeling. I prefer being in my cabin. I also prefer being under the illusion that I was the only female that dared speak. Now, I am further on edge, wondering if the women around me have a secret club and all use their words when they are alone. I wonder if maybe only one of them in this room is part of the secret society. I also wonder if none of them are and they are strong believers of the world we live in. By the time I have finished peeling the potatoes, I have gnawed at my bottom lip so much I can taste the strong coppery tang of fresh blood.

Boots thud against the hard floor, the groaning of the old building following closely behind. All the ladies bow their heads and place their hands behind their backs as the boots near us. I follow suit and stare at my feet that now have soft leather boots over them. I wonder if they are new or if they were owned by someone who has passed from this world.

"Breakfast will be served half an hour earlier than usual so move your asses. There will then be a burial in the forest afterward." Jeremiah's voice breaks through my loud mind. I want to look up and make eye contact. To remind him of our own secret society, but I fight the urge and wiggle my toes.

Once he is done speaking, the women begin gathering piles of plates to take to the common hall. I move to follow but a vise grips my wrist.

"Not you. You eat in your cabin. Or don't." Jeremiah's knuckles turn white as he squeezes my small wrist. I nod once but he doesn't let go. Instead, he pulls on my wrist and leads me from the hall. When we are outside, he scorns me under his breath. "You could have cost that girl her life," he growls.

"What girl?" I mumble, knowing damn well who he is talking about. His grip becomes painful. Deadly. My fingers tingle and burn as the circulation in my hand is cut off.

"Well no matter, your interference now means she will be watched closely."

I frown and side eye him as we step up to my cabin. He pushes the door open and rips me through the threshold.

"What do you mean closely?"

He snickers and runs a lone fingertip along the edge of my jawline. My skin erupts into goosebumps.

"She's on bedrest. Indefinitely until she produces an offspring for her husband. The doctor scraped her uterus clean and the dead fetus along with its poisoned blood will be buried where your brother is."

Bile rises to my throat. "You can't keep her on bedrest. What if she doesn't get pregnant right away?" I ask as the severity of the situation settles in.

Jeremiah leans in close, his breath brushing my earlobe. "Yeah, she will be chained to a bed for the rest of her fucking existence. Next time you want to act like a savior or fucking god, remember where you are! There are no fucking saviors in this world!" His voice rises on the last sentence.

I shiver and pull away from him. He lets me and steps back, creating an icy cold feeling between us. "Please don't do that to her," I say softly.

He tilts his head and looks over me coldly. Then turns to leave, gripping the door handle behind him.

"I wanted to kill him before. Now I will make it painful. That's my promise."

He pauses with my door only slightly ajar now.

"The problem with me, is I don't know if I hate you so much I want to kill you or fuck you till you bleed. You are getting cocky, confident and fucking stupid. I think it will end in me hating you so much I will kill you."

The door slams shut behind him and I sink to the ground. I fear he is right. He may very well be the one that will end my life. I have always known it deep down. My soul has always known it and has feared him for as long as I have known him.

I just need to kill everyone on my list first.

CHAPTER 22

W hen the night comes again, I do not know what to expect. Or who.

My mind spins like crazy as the goal I desperately hope to achieve before I meet my maker seems to move further and further away. If Aurelia is on bedrest, I need to find out where. She will either be in their homestead or in the doctor's clinic. A shiver involuntary spreads over my body and leaves me feeling chilled to the bone. She will be tied to a bed for years. If she gets pregnant instantly and is lucky, it may only be one year. But it could also take her a long time to get pregnant again and she won't be off bedrest until after the baby's safe arrival. I swallow thickly and shake my head. *Huh, safe arrival into the pits of hell.*

I eye the door that hasn't been locked yet carefully. Could I stop all of this? I have tried to play the martyr before and it backfired, but if I take away the root of the problem then there is no way it can backfire.

I turn and go to the shelf across the small space that holds the ingredients I have saved for a rainy day. It may not be raining, and it is no longer day but let's not let semantics spoil things.

My fingers brush the cold glass jar as my door opens. A small yelp bursts from me and I lurch away from my shelf. Jeremiah shuts the door behind him and looks me up and down. His accusing eyes drag slowly over every part of me, leaving me feeling nervous yet excited. Does he know? I brush away loose strands of hair from my face and tuck it behind my ears.

Tilting his head, he scowls. "What are you up to?"

"Me?" My voice comes out on a squeak. *Fuck.*

He pointedly looks around the room before his eyes land back on me. "Well, doesn't seem like I would be asking anybody else, would it?" he bites out.

"I'm not doing anything. I am stuck in a cabin, remember?"

"Memory serves that you prefer to be alone in this cabin."

"What do you want?" I ask quickly. Jeremiah and I do not hold conversations with each other. It's starting to make me feel uncomfortable. I would prefer him to beat me with a barbed wire bat than talk to me.

"Are you going to tell me what you are up to?" he asks again. Fuck.

"You're paranoid," I reply hastily.

He lets out a long sigh and steps closer to me. It's only then that I notice he has a large oil skin satchel in his hand.

"I am many things, dear Violet. Paranoid is not one of them. I am very intuitive, I am logical and I am not fucking stupid."

"Well I am sure you will lock the door when you leave so what can I really be up to apart from being stuck in my fucking cabin?" I burst out. Standing here, in this abnormal conversation with Jeremiah, makes me realize his voice has a husky undertone to it. The roughness of it matches his hand, his way of being. Yet the graveling tone in it also soothes, almost like it's naturally coaxing the truth off my tongue.

Phoenix has a smooth, velvety voice. Yin and yang in all ways.

"Don't raise your voice to me ever again, Violet." His eyes narrow and burn straight into my own. Why is this more painful and excruciating to me?

"What's that?" I ask quietly and jerk my chin to the satchel. If I take a step away from Jeremiah, will he notice? Being this close to him, in his headlights, is distracting me from how I really wanted to spend my night. Or well, so I thought. Now I really want to lie flat on my back while he makes me feel pain in more than one way.

If he asks me to, I will drop to my knees and crawl to him. I hope he doesn't ask me to.

As if he had nearly forgotten, he follows my line of sight to his bag. He raises his eyebrows and a subtle smirk plays at the corner of his mouth.

He steps around me and stops at the work bench so his back is turned to me. He lifts the satchel and places the contents of the bag on the bench. There's a soft knock as the item makes contact with the hard wood. My heart pounds painfully against my rib cage from the anticipation. He steps away from the bench and faces me.

My loud gasp fills the room, bouncing off the walls in the thickly tense room. I cover my mouth with my sweaty hand and choke on my words. "Wha-why—" But the shock morphs into vomit when the smell reaches my nose.

I turn my head and empty my stomach contents onto the floor. I wipe my lips with the back of my hand and look back at Jeremiah. I can't bring myself to look at what is sitting on my work bench. His face is furious, as if he wasn't expecting this reaction.

I can only breathe out one word. "Why?" The single word still carries my sickened feeling.

A deep frown settles above his eyes as he crosses his arms over his chest, causing his shirt to bunch under his forearms.

"You said I don't do anything nice. So this is me trying to be nice!" he growls. My eyes widen when I realize he is being dead serious.

"This is nice? What even the fuck is that?" I ask and wave my hand to the deformed and rotting object.

"Is it not obvious what it fucking is?"

"Yeah but also not really."

Slowly, I peel my eyes off him and back down to the gray shaded cock on my work bench. Parts of the flesh are rotting. Or were, at least before it was stuffed.

The dead, stinking cock sits on a wooden, circular piece of wood, like a trophy.

"You should recognize it easily. You cut it from your brother's fucking body. I thought you might like it. It's my first time trying taxidermy. You could be a little more grateful."

I step back, away from my brother's dick. He cannot be serious right now. He pushes off the work bench and storms to the door.

"Last time I try to be fucking *nice.*" He spits the last word out as if it is even painful to say. "You are fucking with my head, I don't know why I give two shits about how you fucking feel. You're nothing more than a slave in our kingdom. Maybe you are more trouble than you are worth. Pussy is pussy at the end of the day. As for that—" He dips his head to my brother's cock. "Do what you want with it. Sit on it for all I fucking care," he roars and slams the door behind him. In his anger, he doesn't lock the door. I can hear the sound of his thudding boots getting quieter the further he storms away.

I look back to the cock and slowly creep closer to it. I can't help it. I run a finger over the deformed tip before I rip my hand back instantly. It feels like leather and it moves slightly under my finger. He didn't do it right because I think it's meant to be completely hard. It's not old rotted skin—it's still slowly rotting. I pinch my fingers around the wood panel and step outside to throw the rotting flesh underneath my cabin.

I move back into the cabin, still reeling from what has just transpired. *A slave in their kingdom?*

He has firmly reminded me why I need to stay focused on my goal. I need to burn their fucking kingdom to the ground.

I snag a glass jar of poisonous dried berries from my shelf and pull my black hooded gown from its hook, throwing it over myself. I place one of my herb knives into my waistband and leave my dark cabin. The door creaks and clicks shut behind me. I make my way through the dark village, careful to stick to the shadows. I know exactly the cabin I need to get to. I smile to myself the closer I get. I feel like the grim fucking reaper.

CHAPTER 23

I arrive at their small abode and nestle myself under the window to the main room, with my back flat against the exterior wall. I hear soft creaking of the wooden floorboards but no speaking. My fingertips dig into patches of moss that coat the outside. I'm not nervous, I am growing impatient. I have a plan, but it's not really a plan. I am going to kill the putrid man that lives in this house. But other details are yet to be decided.

I hear a door open and then shut. Sucking in a deep breath, I hold it with my heart pounding against my ribs at a dangerous rate. The floorboards still creak and groan but it's now slightly further away. I take the risk and stretch up to the window frame, fingers clenching around the wooden frame before pulling myself up as much as possible. I manage to stretch just enough to spy over the frame.

The room is dimly lit with nothing but a lantern in the far corner, positioned on a small wooden dining table. There is a circular stool pushed under it, with three worn looking legs coming off the seat.

Cunt must make his beautiful wife sit on the floor. Or maybe she is not allowed to sit at all. Looking toward the closed bedroom door, I realize this may be my only chance.

"Seems plan enough to me," I whisper to myself.

I creep around to the front door, quietly not slowly. I don't know how much time I have. Gingerly, I tiptoe onto the porch and place my fingers on the round door handle. I close my eyes and blow a long slow breath out before I turn the handle. Fear grips me as a subtle squeak sounds when the knob turns. I hear a soft click and push the door open, just enough that I can slip through. Pushing the door shut behind me, I press my head and back against the door, refusing to take my eyes off the bedroom door. I wait momentarily and force myself to move once more. My hand grips the jar of poison with force as my eyes roam around the main living quarters. My eyes land on a tall mason jar with homemade rum in it. There is a half-eaten boiled egg beside it on a ceramic saucer. I move toward it and take the jar lid off, but as I tip the contents, sounds of thumping comes from the other room. I pause, staring at the wall separating myself from the monster. My wide eyes turn to a disgruntled frown when the banging becomes more rhythmic.

"Let the gods nourish my seed inside my chosen vessel," he grunts loudly and his thrusts gain in pace.

Motherfucker is fucking her right now.

I grow angrier, knowing she must be chained beneath him. I tap the contents into the jar and use my finger to stir it around before I wipe my hand on my gown. I have overdone it, but I want him to die quickly.

I leave the quarters and resume my position under the window. Looking around into the darkness, I eye the other homes, but I know I haven't been spotted. There would have been a full-blown ruckus by now.

Movement becomes evident and very slowly, I drag myself up and peer over the frame. He sits down on his stool and kicks his feet out in front of him. He wears nothing but his trunks and it makes me want to gag more. Sick fuck. My eyes slide toward the now open bedroom door and I see Aurelia lying flat on her back with a pillow underneath her hips. Her hands are unbound and she rubs her wrists slowly, looking completely defeated. Her lower lip is bloodied and her right eye is rimmed with blue and black bruising. I hate him. With all my might.

The man takes a long pull on the rum and sets it back down. Following a burp, he says, "Two more minutes with the pillow then you get tied back up."

He scratches his chin and slowly moves his hand up along his jaw, running through it with his fingers.

He picks up his jar of rum again and I lean in by stretching on my toes, just scraping the damp grass beneath me. Too eager for his demise, I slip and my forehead knocks against the bottom of the glass panel. His head swivels toward me and we lock eyes instantly. Fuck. I drop down, crouching low beneath the window. I pull my small knife from my waistband as footsteps echo all around me. He moves quickly across his cabin, rips the door open and moves around the building before stopping in front of me. His breaths heave in and out, with his chest rising high with every motion.

"You fucking bitch. Now you are finally giving me reason and perfect opportunity to sever that pathetic head from your body."

"No, it is *you* who dies tonight," I growl beneath my breath.

He hisses and lurches forward, surprising me. He lifts me from the ground with his hands wrapped firmly around my throat. My eyes burn as the pressure from the loss of air becomes too much. His wild eyes bore into mine. One of my hands taps frantically at his determined hold while the other still grips my small herb knife.

He stumbles slightly with me still in his grasp so I take the moment to force my knife up into his ribs. He gasps and lets me go, causing me to collapse to the ground.

"Do you feel that change in your body?" I ask, now staring up into his shocked face.

"You," he breathes.

"That feeling is death coming for you."

There is movement beside us and Aurelia drops to her knees, unable to take her eyes away from what is unfolding.

"Do you feel your heart fighting to pump blood around your body? That is death coming for you," I whisper. He stumbles back a few steps, skin becoming ash-like. I turn my head to Aurelia with a devilish smirk to my lips.

"We do win. See? We don't always have to lose," I boast proudly. "Don't drink the rum. Tip it out," I say sternly this time and turn back to my latest victim. I crawl toward him and he drops to his knees. One hand clutches his chest as the other presses against his fresh wound. I crawl on top of him, straddling him angrily.

Without second thought, I stab my small knife directly into his heart and lean in close, whispering into his ear, "And death is me."

His eyes glaze over, the sparkle of life draining away so now there is dull nothingness.

I take a quick glance at my wet knees that are dug into the ground on either side of his hips. Slowly, I stand up, never taking my eyes off the corpse. I raise my hand slowly, holding it above the body and peel my eyes away so I can look at my bloodied fingers. So still. Not a single tremor runs through my body. Should I be sad? Nervous? No, all I feel is satisfaction.

I step over him, not bothering to try to hide the body. Let him be found. Or maybe mother nature will high five me and send a black bear to drag him away into the night.

I turn around, expecting to find Aurelia next to me but she's gone. I walk back into the cabin to find her, determined to help her hide this. I helped her. Twice.

Maybe I can tie her back up on the bed so she is safe from suspicion. How could she know anything if she was bedbound?

A loud creak echoes off the walls when I push the door open and step inside. My eyes crawl around the space in front of me as I try to find her. The lantern's light flickers and bounces shadows on the wooden walls. That's when I see her bare feet. Flat on the ground, off the side of the bed.

"Hey I have a plan," I tell her but I get no answer. I shouldn't be surprised.

Her gown flutters around her knees but I can't see the rest of her. She must be leaning back against her headboard.

I stroll closer, but pause when I find myself in the doorway with Aurelia completely in my view now. A thud fills the room and an uncontrollable cry escapes me. "Why?" I gasp in agony and disbelief.

I slide my eyes to the empty jar that's fallen to the ground and then back to Aurelia's sullen face. She wipes the back of her hand across her wet lips and lifts her legs and lies down on the bed. She closes her eyes, refusing to look at me but a lone tear falls from her eyes and rolls down her temples onto the pillow beneath her.

"Because it will just be someone else. With him gone, it means another will take me. There are no victories in a place like this."

I want to tell her if I force my fingers down her throat and make her throw up, I could still save her. It's a slim chance. But a chance all the same. But as I open my mouth to demand she let me, my airways are cut off. Pain tears at my neck as my lungs fight for air that cannot come.

"You have made the decision for me. Maybe you wanted me to kill you all along."

Jeremiah's vicious voice is the last thing I hear.

CHAPTER 24

The smell of thick dust and rusty metal is offensive to my nose. I try to sit up but my body is bound flat on my back and my eyes are still swollen shut, struggling to open. I flex my fingers in and out a few times before clenching them tightly into fists. My mouth is painfully dry. My tongue sticks to the roof of my mouth and the more I try to move it around, the more it feels like coarse sandpaper.

"Did you bury both the bodies?" I hear Phoenix ask Jeremiah. He sounds close.

"Yeah right next to her brother. We going with the *they escaped story* still?"

I hear scratching and finally pry my eyes open. My gritty eyes land on Phoenix, watching him as he scratches the stubble on his chin. He catches my stare and stares back at me. I don't know what to think right now, I am every bit their prisoner. That has become clear. But the more he watches me, the more I become confused with the outcome of my prisoner life.

Without taking his eyes off me, he answers, "Yeah, might need to have another one *escape* too."

Jeremiah walks around the platform I am on and stands shoulder to shoulder with Phoenix. He crosses his arms over his large chest and narrows his gaze on me. "Oh you're awake," he states angrily.

"Just fucking kill me," I rasp out. My throat burns, causing my voice to sound hoarse.

Jeremiah steps forward, closing the distance between us. Too close. This isn't turning me on anymore. My body doesn't become hot with need and yearning for his wicked hands to be on me.

He places his hands on the bench surface now, leaning his body weight on his hands as his eyes crawl over my bare skin. It's only now I realize I am completely naked. More in tune to my body, I now feel the shift in the wind and the assault of the cold night breeze licking painfully at my body.

My toes flex in and out at the uncomfortable and somewhat painful feeling. The rest of me is tied down. My shoulders shift from side to side as much as they can but I could probably only move a few inches.

As I lie here, under the scrutiny of his furious stare, I can't help but reflect on the last few weeks. It's like a time-lapse recording playing at rapid speed behind my eyes. My brother taking a part of me I never expected, turning my once picturesque breasts into scabbed wounds on the front of my chest. Burying someone alive, killing multiple people. Playing the heroine yet becoming the villain.

But most of all in a short time, going from thinking the two men beside me were the scariest humans that walked this earth to now thinking I could be their equal. I'm tainted now. I thought I could be different and escape this treacherous hell without becoming like them. But this fucking place sucks you in and morphs you into a monster no matter how hard you try to fight it.

"You know, you could have been great. We could have been great, all together," Jeremiah says, following a loud, irritated sigh.

Phoenix now joins him, once again standing shoulder to shoulder with him.

"I thought the way my body only reacted to you, that it must mean I was only meant for you. You are right, Jeremiah. I had hope for a future with us flipping this place around and starting our own beliefs. The three of us starting a new movement. But you really had to fuck it up big time, Violet."

I don't respond straight away. Weeks ago, their words would've wounded me deeply. I would've shivered and shied away, petrified of these men. But the fear is gone now.

Finally, I swallow and speak. "You know. You think that you used me. Lucky little Violet gets some attention. She should be grateful. She should be submissive. You both used me for your own needs. Phoenix, you finally got your cock hard so you decided to fuck me as much as possible and I should be grateful the leader is fucking me and not beating me. Jeremiah is a big scary guard that falls asleep dreaming of pulling people limb by limb and found a female that isn't squeamish and can be his torture partner. Lucky me, getting used by you both. But did you ever think I was playing you both?"

Phoenix side eyes Jeremiah and squeezes his hands into tight fists. Jeremiah stands tall, strong, with his arms still firmly across his chest.

"Long ago, I swore I would kill you all," I whisper. "The only way I was ever going to get the opportunity to kill more of the monsters here was to play along with getting fucked by you both. I mean sure, the fucking was quite enjoyable but the biggest success was when you both got distracted and kept my cabin unlocked, when you got comfortable and complacent, thinking I wasn't going anywhere because I am so *fucking grateful.* The only thing I regret is not killing more of you, but oh well, I let my anger get the better of me."

Jeremiah's face falters. Going from poised yet lethal to surprised. A new look soon settles over his face, though. Almost like a demon has risen to the surface, darkening his eyes.

"So what, we were a means to an end?" Jeremiah spits through his clenched teeth. Oh scary Jeremiah is coming back out to play.

"Yep! Now just kill me," I reply but there's a sting deep inside me that settles heavy in my chest when I answer him. I really did enjoy fucking them both. Sharing my mutilated body with their rough hands. Burying my brother late at night and sharing our secret moments. I don't think I ever wanted to admit that to myself so I ignored the comfort I was beginning to feel around them. But now I remain strong and stare up to the ceiling. I refuse to ponder on my possible regret and the what ifs that I could like it here. What if I had just succumbed to my psychotic feelings and stopped pretending I was a good person? Jeremiah believes every word I spoke. I am not surprised. I did believe them up until about a minute ago.

He leans down, his hot breath coating my ear. "Did I ever tell you? I have always wanted to kill you?" he growls quietly. He has. Long ago when he first said it and he reminded me frequently ever since.

"But fast is not my forte," he says absently as he walks toward a wooden bench full of tools and instruments. We are back in the shed where I have seen many tortured.

Phoenix steps back, leaning one shoulder against the wall. His eyes dart between Jeremiah plucking tools off the wooden bench and my scarred body lying flat on the bench.

Being beaten, sliced and tortured was always a fear of mine. Not the death at the end, but living through endless physical pain. I don't know if I can be brave. Slowly, I close my eyes and search my mind for that place where no pain and hurt can find me.

The pain of the first slice causes me to throw my eyes open and let a pained gasp rip from my throat. How I pictured it would feel is exactly how it is. Maybe worse.

I can't move. I can't run away and at least hope to escape. *Hope*. That is what is completely missing when every part of your body is tied down and someone is slicing into your tender skin. The mere emotion is what distracts you from the horror and pain you feel. Without hope, there is no distraction, just horror and pain. I feel blood trickle down my bare thigh while the small cut stings.

Jeremiah focuses on the fresh cut, his eyes lit up like he is watching a fireworks display in front of him. He looks so excited, eager to make the display bigger, better, brighter.

Is this how I looked when I was killing my brother and my latest victim?

"Please just kill me. I am okay with death."

He hums for a moment and drags his tongue over his bottom lip. "Death is easy. As easy as it is cutting into your soft flesh."

He is completely lost. I am nothing more than a new canvas to him now. His hand is so still, not a single tremor can be seen. He leans over a little further and slices the other thigh. A little deeper this time. At the same time, he slams a hand down on my mouth so my screech is suffocated into his palm.

Blood spills down my other thigh. Tears roll down the side of my face, causing a spark of anger to ignite. Fuck them. I don't want to look weak but the pain is taking away any choices I have over my emotions and body.

He leans down close to my face so we are nose to nose, and smiles. Using his free arm, he slowly drags the tip of his switch blade down my torso. My sobs rack against his hand but he only smiles wider. He moves down my body and drags his tongue up my fresh cut, taking in as much of my blood as he can. He moves up and looks down into my pained face with my fresh blood on his lips. He swipes his thumb across his lips and swipes his tongue out over them again.

"I don't know what excites me more—your blood or your pussy juice."

The knife he still grips like his life depends on it glides lightly over my thigh, leaving goosebumps everywhere it touches. Tears still stream down my face.

"I hate you."

"I know," he replies. I hear rustling and move my attention toward where Phoenix still silently stands. He shuffles again, looking uncomfortable, eyebrows drawn in deeply and lines deep between them. He is strong, deadly and fucking sick but he's shown me he has a different side. He has shown me kindness. Maybe I can use that.

He draws his eyes from Jeremiah's knife, that still moves over my skin in intricate patterns. He locks eyes with mine and stretches his arms up, brushing his hands over his prickly scalp. His blue eyes show me emotions he may not even realize. Confusion. He doesn't know how he should feel right now. He has obviously never tortured someone he has had sexual relations with.

"Can't you just steal my last breath from me and then carry on your life," I say hoarsely, directing my words at Phoenix. Jeremiah pauses and looks between us. Phoenix doesn't answer but he clears his throat and diverts his gaze.

"Don't talk to him."

"Why? Because I know he has a heart."

"He doesn't have a heart."

"He does. I've seen it. I've experienced it."

Jeremiah scoffs and continues to run the blade over my skin, pushing a little deeper now. It must be so close to breaking my skin. "Probably more deception in your words."

"I have seen a heart from you too. No matter how much we both hide it over our bravado, we felt something. We connected over drawing blood. The only thing is, I accept my actions, I don't regret them and now I am ready to meet my maker. You don't need to slice pieces off me first."

Jeremiah stays silent for just a moment before he slowly digs the knife in further, piercing my skin painfully. I cry out, unable to hold it in even if I wanted to.

"I think you may actually be right. I am a sick, sick man. Man doesn't seem right. Maybe a monster, sadist even. For you, I showed that I can be more than just a person who enjoys seeing how much blood someone has in their body. How many heartbeats they still have while a screwdriver slowly pierces it, inch by inch. And all you did with that was play needless games," he growls out the last bit angrily and drives the knife deeper. Hitting muscle.

"Ahh fu—" I cry out.

Phoenix moves to where I am tied down, hand clasping around Jeremiah's grip. "Enough, I think we have made a point."

"Point? I'm not trying to make a point. I am trying to have some late-night fun."

Phoenix squeezes his hand harder, I am certain I hear cracks. Jeremiah whips his hand out and clenches it around Phoenix's throat. His teeth are clenched together tightly, face turning an angry red. "If you want to keep her as a precious little pet, fuck her."

Phoenix doesn't answer. He can't. He just drops his gaze to me.

"Fuck her right here, right now and I will make her death quick. Refuse then I will take that as the sign you don't give two fucks about her and will keep slicing bits off her until there is nothing left."

CHAPTER 25

I want to say Phoenix rode in as my knight in shining armor. I want to say he's the strong leader I have always known him to be and he put an end to Jeremiah's antics. That isn't the case though. Whatever Phoenix may or may not feel for me, he has been born and raised in this fucked up place. Blood, torture and now fresh sex are just too tempting to pass up. I know he had an issue with sex in the past. He came to me to rectify it, and I ended up helping him rectify it in a much more intimate way.

His hard cock bulges against his linen slacks. It's hefty, and I wonder if it's painful. I hope it is. I can see the outline of his tip but I am not overcome with desire. I want to be dead or standing over their dead bodies. I turn my head away, making Jeremiah snicker under his breath. He then taps his booted foot on the hard ground, showing us he is impatient and waiting. Phoenix dives right in, playing his part perfectly. Still standing, he hovers over me and grips both sides of my face with his hands and turns it toward him.

"Do I disgust you that much? It was not long ago you would clench around my shaft as you come. Would you rather not have this than have the butcher cut you into pieces?"

"Sorry if I am not hot and bothered right now," I whisper simply, keeping my eyes closed. I hear a sigh of resignation before his hands leave the side of my head and move down my body. He takes his time, fingers spread and palm flat, feeling every part of my body he can.

"How can you be so scarred and so worn from the life you have lived yet be so beautiful. So alive. That's what I am drawn to most. The spark in you is something I envy." His words seem so far away but they find a way to stab at my fragile soul. Not enough to want me to want this though. How could that ever be the case?

His hands move over my still healing breasts. No longer do I feel the sensitive tingle in my core when my breasts are touched by another man. Now it's simply the sensation of any other part of my body. It reminds me of how bravely I took that power back. The brisk winter breeze only adds to the eerie feeling of contempt in the shed. His hands move lower, lightly skimming over my hollow naval before his fingers flutter lower, dancing over my hips. I still don't look. My eyes remain shut and my breathing is even. Is there another part of my body I need to mutilate so it cannot be used against me?

Careful fingertips press down lightly on my groin, sweeping softly over my sensitive lips. Still, I don't feel the heated sensation I have experienced before with Phoenix and Jeremiah. It tickles, but not sexually. His fingers move between my lips, gently rubbing my clit and down to my opening. A soft, breathy groan leaves his lips when his fingers find my warm, damp core.

"Should I be offended that you're not dripping wet for me? Possibly. But I am the devil, remember, I take what I want anyway. Although you should be a little more thankful I am saving you from being Jeremiah's fun toy. His toys usually end up in a fire, or in the forest grave site."

"I think I like him more. I always knew who he was and exactly where I stood with him. I know he likes to be depraved. You...you are like an identity crisis," I whisper, my eyes still squeezed shut.

"You are the one that gives me an identity crisis. I knew who I was until you piqued my interest."

I snort. I can't help it. "I know what part of you piqued with interest."

Phoenix inserts his finger deeper, dragging it in and out of my pussy. It feels like he is pushing against gravity. My pussy is damp but not wet with pleasure. The friction on my walls begins to burn.

"Unbind her ankles," Phoenix orders Jeremiah, who moves. I know because his heavy army boots clomp against the ground. Only now do I open my eyes, watching Jeremiah stand at the foot of the table, a stern expression cast on his face.

He works at the rope around my ankles and drops them free once he is done. He rubs his thumbs over the raw red marks on my tender skin before he spreads my ankles apart. My lips part, making me feel open and exposed. He moves away though and Phoenix takes his place. He drops his pants and puts his knee onto the bench and climbs on to settle between my legs. His erection is hard to miss. Phoenix falters for a moment with a concerned frown on his face. His fingers still work my pussy and I know he is frustrated there is no lubrication.

But he pulls his fingers out and lies flat on me, with one hand pressed just above my shoulder so he can hold his weight just off me. I glance to the side, noting the way his forearm tensed under his weight. We then lock eyes for a moment. More than anything, I feel hurt.

"You are no better than my brother," I tell him quietly. He pauses, faltering once again. *Identity crisis.* Who does he really want to be?

Jeremiah grows impatient and grips Phoenix's raging cock. "Here, let me," he snarls. "It's my favorite knife."

He strokes the cock a few times, gripping it with such an intense force that it turns an angry red. He points it toward my opening and I lean my head back.

"No one uses me and gets away with it," Jeremiah snarls.

It nudges my opening as Jeremiah guides it in. Phoenix doesn't protest. *Be brave, Violet,* I give myself a mental pep talk myself. I remember when I once told myself physical pain was a state of mind that could be ignored.

"Fuck," I hiss as the cock is forced into my protesting vagina. Tears roll down my face and Phoenix tenses on top of me.

"I can't do it," he says close to my face. His voice isn't strong and determined. It's weak and regretful.

"Do it," Jeremiah insists again.

Phoenix pulls back and shoves Jeremiah to the side. He climbs off and puts his pants back on.

"Cut her into pieces, I don't fucking care. But I can't be with her like that," Phoenix bites out and looks over my naked body. I watch him in shock, so sure I can see an uneasy quiver running through his body. I have spent most of my life watching this man hand out punishments, barbaric ones at that. Yet with me, he always seems to be in conflict with his conscience.

"What the fuck has happened to you?" Jeremiah asks him but it seems more like a criticism.

"Maybe she finally made me find my humanity," he replies before he leaves the shed. I squeeze my legs shut, my body now trembling. Jeremiah shakes his head slowly when the shed door slams behind Phoenix. Finally, after staring into the shut door for what felt like countless minutes, he sighs and moves his attention back to me.

"Who knew one single lady could bring our historic cult to an untimely end."

"Kill me and be done with it," I bark at him with more tears streaming down my face.

Absently, Jeremiah walks down the edge of the table I lie on and moves across and up the other side. He walks around slowly, going around and around me. Finally, he stops and side eyes me. "He cares for you. Not something I care to see."

He runs a finger over one of my thigh wounds before continuing, "I wonder if I may to have feelings. But I have this need to draw blood. An addiction to feeling flesh be torn apart. It's a feeling I crave and gravitate toward whenever I have the possibility. That feeling outweighs anything else I may feel." He then digs a fingertip into my wound. I sob loudly and kick my leg out. He holds them down now with a face set in stone. I am at the mercy of a madman.

Jeremiah picks up his blade again and returns to my body. The air between us is thick. Thick with terror and excitement on his behalf. I take a deep breath in and let out a long, slow one through my cracked lips. It hasn't calmed me though. My hands are clammy and my heart pounds against my chest painfully. He presses the tip of his blade to my torso and I let out a defeated cry. It's one of the only parts left on my body that isn't scarred and ruined. He draws the blade across my skin, close to my naval. I whimper and he smiles. His face looks manic, like he isn't really in there anymore. I have seen this first hand before. When we killed my brother. He carves a pattern into my stomach, careful with every single line. Once he is done, he stands up straight, looking down at what he has just done and nods to himself. *He is impressed with his work?* I refuse to look. Maybe now he will kill me.

But to my surprise, he undoes the rope around my wrist closest to him and leans over me, skimming his heaving chest against my own. We lock eyes as he undoes the other wrist.

"I want to fuck you while your wounds bleed. I want your vibrant fresh blood all over my body. I want to use it as lubrication on my cock." He sounds tense. I swallow and turn my head to the side.

"I won't though. Not now, anyhow. You will remember though, how much you liked giving into your animal side and finding pleasure amongst the tortured. How wet it made you feel. How hard it made me watch you cut your brother's cock from his body." He whispers the last part in a pant. "Go," he finishes simply and turns his back to me.

I sit up and rub my wrists then flick my legs off the table and search around for my gown. I reach for it when it's found and pull it around me. I limp out of the shed and head toward my cabin.

I still am alive, and I am still their fucking prisoner.

CHAPTER 26

G ingerly, I shuffle around my small space, finding my flint stones and collection of kindling sticks. I start a small fire and grab my candles to begin lighting them all one by one. I'm frustrated. I am angry. Sore. But I can't let myself believe I am defeated. If I really wanted to die, I could do it myself. I know that. But I want other people's deaths before my own, and I am gutless in wanting someone else to kill me.

I can't help but fall to my knees when I am done in sheer agony but also helplessness. I don't know what is hurting me more. The fact my anger got the better of me and I barely completed the entire task I had in my head, or the fact that when I said I feel nothing for the two men, I felt a pang of guilt and pain. I *do* feel something. Something different in them both but a need for them, nonetheless. When Jeremiah said I need to give into my animal instincts, I felt something warm in me. It's like a switch that can go off.

I run my fingers over my thighs, leaving marks in the wet blood. Slowly, I move my hands up and run my fingers over my stomach. I shuffle closer to one of the flickering candles and look down to finally see what pattern Jeremiah carved into me. But it's not a pattern. I gasp and frown deeply while I read over the letters again. *Ours.*

Theirs? Why do I feel some sort of comfort for this dominating brand now etched into my body? My windows shake as the eerie cold night wind howls out through the trees. I reach for the cloth under the bench that I usually make satchels out of and tear it into strips. One after the other, I wrap the cloth around my thighs, securing the ends tightly. I need to stitch them up, but I don't have any thin needles on me. My last one was used on my nipples and then disposed of. I don't want to use my satchel stitching needles I made out of wood to pull my flesh together. I use my water jug and leftover cloth to wipe the blood from the rest of my thighs and clean my stomach.

I pull a tunic over myself and crawl into bed, wrapping my fur blanket tightly around myself. I huddle myself into a ball and let the tears flow. I don't tell myself to be brave or to feel ashamed or weak for crying. I let this be closure. I cry for the woman that lost her baby and her life. It's what she wanted but the heaviness on me doesn't lessen because of that. I cry for the little girl I once was that had a mother, although loyal to our own cult, who I felt loved me. I cry for the adults in our last cult that promised the little girl in me that I would be taken to a much better place, only to be left behind. I cry hard and ugly. And I don't stop until sleep finally consumes me. My last thought to myself before sleep encapsulates me is that these will be the last tears I cry.

When the next morning comes, I honestly do not know what to expect. I feel worn and on edge. My garments were soaked through with blood when I woke, but thankfully the bleeding seems to have stopped.

I put on my warmer outer garments and patiently wait. I hear footsteps before one of the women comes in. My eyes widen from the unexpected shock when she places a bowl of hot porridge down on the floor just past the threshold. She says nothing, which is not unexpected, and shuts the door behind her. This has never happened before.

Limping over to the porridge, I pick it up and begin to eat it on the edge of my cot. There is a soft yet constant shake in my body. I am completely drained physically and emotionally. When I put the small wooden spoon of oats into my mouth, my dull hair falls over my shoulder, threatening to touch the breakfast contents. I shrug my shoulders back, moving my hair away from the bowl. I sigh and place the bowl beside me and rest my hands on my lap. My fingers tremble when I begin picking at my rough nails. As much as I try not to think of life outside of this cult, it is really hard not to. Women can speak freely; they play roles of dominance in some situations. They live a life of true freedom. I want that so badly but as I glance down over my ravaged body, I sigh with the realization it may just be too late for me. The chance of me being one of those lucky ones that get away is so slim. Slimmer than slim. I wanted so much more, and I also wanted death. I yearned and dreamed of a brighter life, but I knew the only way I would escape this hellhole is through death.

By the time I am done fighting back my unshed tears for my perilous life, I have made my nail beds bleed. I shake my hands and lift the warm bowl of porridge again and force myself to eat more. I need to dig deep and fuel my determination to find an end to this place. I need to suck up the dwellings of my own shitty life and help create a future for the next generation, at least. Maybe then I could escape the unfair emotions over my fucked-up life for what it has been and what it will remain to be. I don't think I will ever venture over these mountains or through the forest to find a new civilization. But I could possibly find peace in helping some find that freedom. Couldn't I?

I look up through my eyelashes at the front door. The voices on the other side of it are low and deep but it catches my attention all the same. I tense and place my bowl down once again. The voices don't belong to Jeremiah and Phoenix. I bite my bottom lip and stand, shuffling back and not taking my eyes off the door. The hairs on the nape of my neck begin to stand on end and my skin prickles painfully. At first, I was criticizing myself for knowing the tone of Jeremiah and Phoenix's voices, but now I am growing wary. Something feels off.

My back touches the wooden bench and I feel around with my hands, trying to find a weapon but my hands slide around fruitlessly. The door finally opens, ever so slowly. The creak of the hinges is long and loud. It makes it seem more sinister. Once it is fully opened, it thuds against the wooden wall and in the threshold stands three large men. I have seen them around. They are on the council. But I have never had anything to do with them.

One by one, they step inside my small space, now making me feel claustrophobic and suffocated. My heart races and bile burns the back of my throat. Their faces say everything I need to know. They are not here to be friendly. The cold wind that tailed them and chilled my bones matches the malice held in their eyes.

"You..." the one at the front says. His ear-length hair is brushed back away from his face. His nose is pointed and his eyebrows are thick. His confident face and straight shoulders tell me he means business.

Be brave, Violet. The single line I have told myself many times. The single line that has stopped my mind from breaking time and time again.

"Me?" I say. The one to the left opens his mouth in shock before it turns downward in an angry frown.

"Yes you...Law breaker. A reject that should never have even been allowed to breathe the same air as us. Your time has come to an end."

"I doubt that. Unless Phoenix says so?" I counter.

He scoffs at my words and cracks his knuckles while looking me up and down with his devious eyes.

"Phoenix is out. As of tomorrow night when we force him out. We see everything. The late-night visits and the missing villagers. You are to blame for all of it. You have poisoned Phoenix. You are both poison that needs to be sucked out and rid of."

"Many have come before you and tried to rid me of this world. Somehow I survive. Somehow I win. Every single time," I say confidently but my insides are in knots. He steps closer to me with a wicked smirk pulling at one side of his mouth.

"Not this time."

His fist comes up in a flash and slams into the side of my head. My neck snaps to the side and I drop to the ground, landing on all fours with a thud. I suck in a chest burning breath with a loud gasp and stay in this painful position, panting heavily. I work my jaw from side to side as a loud ringing fills my ears. Before I can really get a grip on my situation, three pairs of boots stomp closer to me, surrounding me like a cage. I don't know who delivers the first blow but it happens quickly and straight up into my stomach. The wind is instantly knocked out of me, causing me to drop onto the ground. I curl into the fetal position and hug myself tightly while still fighting for air. My hair blankets my face so all I have around me is darkness. Breathing feels like an impossible task but I suck in as much air as I can.

Another hit comes, connecting forcefully against my arms, then another on my back. I hold my body as tight as possible, trying to protect the more vulnerable parts. There's blow after blow until I'm left with nothing but full-body pain that feels like a hand squeezing the life out of me and crushing my bones into dust.

"Enough," a deep voice commands. The brutality stops but I don't feel thankful. I lie in the same position with a fragment of my consciousness left but it's fading. Floorboards creak as the man bends down. I try to move my eyes to show him I am still here. But I can't do anything. I just lie there, hoping my lungs and heart will keep going.

"She lives. We will leave her alive. Tomorrow night she can be burned on the stake with Phoenix. Kind of poetic, isn't it," he says casually. Like this is your average dad joke.

They leave and lock the door behind them. The rusty lock clicks into place and I am once again alone. I can't even cry. I can do nothing but hold on to my last flutters of will to live. I cling to them.

"Your only mistake will be leaving me alive..." I whisper softly, a gargled groan slipping out of me. Finally, I give into the weighted blanket of unconsciousness.

I gasp in pain when my body is lifted off the ground. I am in complete darkness aside from a soft lantern in the corner of my cabin. I can only make out basic colors around me. I am sore all over and a whimper escapes my bloodied lips when I am placed down on my soft cot. I can smell blood all around me, and I can taste the coppery liquid. I let my heavy lids fall completely. I don't care who is moving me. Does it even matter at this point?

I can hear the trickle of water as rags are squeezed out and then slowly, my gown is cut away from my body. The warm, wet cloth runs over my thighs, delicately yet still purposeful. As the cloth is dragged over my wounds on my thigh, I hiss, but I can no longer fight back. My body won't move.

"Shhhh," a deep voice tries to placate me.

"...Hurts," is the only jumbled word I can get out.

"Normally I like seeing bruises and skin after it has been beaten. Now though?" There is a pause in his words as he rinses the rag and swipes it over me again. "Now I feel broken. I am sorry for what I did to you. And I am sorry for what they did to you. I can only put it down to the most human feeling I have ever experienced. And I don't think I like it."

Jeremiah. His voice sounds so concerned. I try to picture what his solemn face looks like as it looks over my body. Then I try to picture an image of my body through his eyes. It only leaves me with fresh tears slipping from my swollen, shut eyes.

"I-I asked you to just kill me," I force out through my closed teeth. But even that hurts. My teeth feel loose and my jaw refuses to move the way it should.

"I can't. I fucking can't, Violet. I should have. A long time ago. Yet I can never do it," he barks and drops his rag into the water. I hear the splash and sigh.

"They know about Phoenix, but not me. I will figure this out. I will get you out of this."

"Look at me. My time has come. Just let me die."

"I'm sorry, Violet. I am fucking selfish, I know. But I can't let you die before me." He pulls the blanket over me and presses something against my mouth. "Open. I need you strong. Nothing is broken. You will heal," he says. I obey and open my mouth. He slips in some pills and presses something to my mouth. Liquid spills against my lips and down my neck. I try to swallow some and force the pills down. Jeremiah stands and retreats to the door, his footsteps moving away from me.

CHAPTER 27

Rain pelts at my small window. It's the first thing my senses tune into when I start to become coherent again.

The wooden window frame rattles under the wind's violent assault. Another storm is brewing. Well no, it's not brewing, it's here causing havoc already. Slowly, I lift my eyelids although they are still reluctant. Once my eyes obey my thoughts and stay open, I stare at the tattered ceiling. The scatters of rotting wood in the joints give me something to focus on momentarily before I find the courage to look over my body. Would I even be able to move enough to look over myself? I fell asleep in the same position I was placed in and that is how I remain now. My tongue gently presses against my tooth that feels too loose in my swollen gums before it runs over it and swipes my bottom lip. My tongue is met with a crusted, dry coating and slight stinging. I don't know if it's blood or a graze starting to scab, probably both now I think about it. I am glad I don't have mirrors around me; my reflection would just show me more of the horror I have been through and the consequences of the venom I spit every chance I get.

I wiggle my toes, deciding to start with the smaller limbs that I doubt were hurt. *Check, toes are safe.* My dark humor seeps through, diluting the reality of my dire situation.

I roll each ankle and pain emerges up my calf muscles, settling deep into my muscles and bones. After moving my head from side to side and deciding I also have a pounding headache, I move my arms under the blankets. The pain is excruciating. Nothing may be broken but it doesn't stop me from feeling like I have shattered glass filling my body, cutting and piercing me every time I breathe or move. As I smooth my hand over my aching ribs and stomach, I curse the three men that thought physically beating me would result in having power over me. They think because they are bigger and stronger that it means they can take leadership of our village.

They think that burning me alive with Phoenix is the worst thing that can happen to me? The worst things have already happened to me over my lifetime.

I think back to when I was younger, eleven years old at most. Thinking I was alone in the garden when I was told I had to gather herbs to hang and dry for the kitchen supply. The glee I felt when I pressed my toes into the topsoil and felt the sunshine over my face.

Looking up toward the sun, the heat radiated against my young skin, making me smile to myself. I forgot myself. I forgot where I was. I was lost in the euphoria and high of freedom. The most freedom I had had since being here and the most freedom I would ever get.

I looked back down over the herbs and plucked the twigs off at the base, sprigs of fresh rosemary, thyme, oregano and basil creating a nice pile in my basket. A soft lullaby passed my lips, so quietly yet peacefully. I made it up as I went. Mentioning the birds, the warm sun, the fresh air that carried the smell of the trees and mountain tops with it. Outside was better than my dark, smelly cabin. It was better than the corner I curled up on with a blanket totally wrapped around me like a cocoon. Father snoring in the far corner on the cot with my brother not far from his side. More of this would be nice. I remember singing to myself in my mind while soft humming continued now my lips were closed.

The pain followed quickly. The only thing I managed was half of a gasp before even that was cut off. My hair was ripped backward from Phoenix's father, the leader at the time. It was brutal with my scalp losing half my hair and the other half barely holding on.

"Ohhh you little cunt. You like the sun, do you? Do you really like the pretty flowers around you? Do you think on your own, do you?" he snarled against my ear. My mousy brown hair stuck to his long gray beard. It's a vision that will always stay looming in my mind. Because his rank breath and flying spit fired poisonous, hateful words into my small ear, while all I could do was look at my tangled hair.

He dragged me back so I lost balance and slumped against his legs. He pulled me over the dirt, my hair still tight in his fist, the only thing connecting us together. I raised my hands and gripped my head tightly because I feared my hair was going to all be ripped out. My eyes began stinging and my clothes were completely soiled from dirt and grass stains as he quickly moved me further toward the large shed. He pulled the door open after we abruptly stopped in front of the shed. With a loud bang when it hit the wall, he ripped me through the threshold. His grip loosened on my ponytail so I looked around a little and started screaming. Ropes and chains hung from the rafters. Butcher tools were scattered over benches and hanging off thick nails in the wooden walls. The shed surroundings were cut off when he squatted down in front of me. His red seething face was all I could see then. His eyes narrowed and lips thinned into white lines. His red neck peeked out from his white linen long sleeve.

"You will always be kept as a lesson. You will be the one that keeps my people in line. You will feel true pain so you never speak again." His words were so lethal I swear I felt like I was already in pain. I sobbed hysterically and begged him for forgiveness. But it only enraged him more. His large, calloused hand connected with my soft, small neck and he squeezed brutally so I could beg no more.

I don't want to die. I want my mom. Please Mommy, come back and save me. Luca? Will he barge through the doors and take me to a place of peace like he always promised? Please someone help me. I don't want to be in pain. I don't want to die. Will anyone help me?

No one came in though. No one interrupted us when he threw my small body against a thick timber pillar. As soon as my back connected with the wood, I urinated through my dirty pants. The liquid ran down my legs, dripping onto the dry dirt beneath me. It only stayed warm for a brief moment before it started to turn cooler. I shivered, the shaking uncontrollable. Not from the cold piss, but from the fear consuming me. I breathed air, yet it felt like I was suffocating.

I shook my head from side to side as soon as he let my neck go but it was no use. He leaned down and picked up a dirty bamboo stick off the ground. Dry, crusted blood coated nearly half of it.

"No, no, no," I repeated over and over. More malice followed my words. He gripped my shoulder, whipping me around and shoving me head first against the pillar.

"I will whip you until no more words leave that disgusting little mouth," he snarled.

He lifted my shirt and pulled it over my head, but not the entire way. The back of it was stuck over the back of my head, holding it up so my bare back was to him. The first lashing came fast and hard. I screamed and begged more. Two more lashings followed, harder than the first. "Please...someone help me," I cried out at the top of my lungs.

No one came that day and my words didn't stop coming until my back was bleeding and my skin was sticking to the bamboo stick before falling onto the dusty ground. My pants filled with urine and feces. I wondered if my rib cage bones were showing.

I remember him finally stopping when I collapsed to the ground, words and sobs no longer possible from me. That would require too much energy. I thought I was about to die. But instead, I remember the words, "Crawl..." leaving his furious mouth. I did what I was told. I crawled from the shed all the way to my cabin. It took hours. But I did it. My father and brother didn't help me through the door. I climbed the two steps and collapsed in my corner like a dog. The trembles came thick and fast, and it took weeks of healing for me to move normally again.

I keep rubbing my ribs as I remember the last of that tortuous period in my life. I saved myself that day. No one came for me. I saved myself and every day after that, I saved myself. That was also the day that made me comfortable in my dark smelly cabin. I no longer had desires to be a part of the village. I was happy when everyone left me alone. I was alone, surviving and safe from those brutal men.

I shift slightly, the old scars on my back feeling like they have come to life all of a sudden and are itchy. It wasn't just the physical pain that made that day the worst day of my life. It was the first day I truly thought I was facing death. It was the realization as a small child that no one will ever save me, and no one will ever care for me. I was utterly alone in this life of mine. Haunted from my family and cults' past mistakes to live a life that is just as haunted.

Physical pain and death threats since that day never hurt as much. They never made me as fearful. Not like that.

Jeremiah steps into my cabin, intruding on me as I relive my past. But he brings things I need. I will save myself again or face death with a smile on my face, but I won't say no to him helping me prior to that. He crouches low so we are eye to eye. I turn my head to him but I don't move any other part of me. He winces and diverts his usually stubborn gaze to the satchel in his hands. I must look as bad as I feel.

"I can't stay here long. Here, take these." He shoves pills against my lips and I open my pained lips. The pills stick to my dry tongue, resting just on the tip.

His eyes dip to them before he drags them back to my battered eyes. "I most definitely am a monster because your tongue still looks incredibly delicious," he whispers, more to himself, and places a flask of water against my lips. I swallow what I can, but the difficult task leaves cold water dribbling down my neck.

"Why don't you just run away? You know the way out. Surely you don't like this life anymore," I ask him quietly, my voice still raspy.

His face holds a sad look before he gives me a soft smile that only makes him look sadder.

"When I say the outside world isn't made for us, I do truly mean it. I don't want to stay here necessarily, but I also don't want to be out there. Everything is fast and loud. Multiple conversations happen at once and they can make your head spin. Their laws and consequences don't make sense. They have a thing called jail that holds men that should be dead. People can steal what they want from one another and only have to pay money to a court if they get fined, and that's only if they even get caught. Our laws are harsh and don't make sense, but out there? It's unruly in a different way," he snickers and takes a cap off another metal flask. "I wouldn't last long out there at all."

He pushes the rim to my lips, the smell of hot broth filling my nose as the steam carries it out of the bottle. I open my mouth and drink as much as I can before he pulls the bottle away from me.

"Sleep, the pills will knock you out for a bit. I will try to get you out before the ceremony tonight." He stands and places the flask into his bag.

"And Phoenix?"

"I am working on it," he confirms but he's already leaving the cabin. The door shuts behind him and the rattle of the lock is followed by a click when he locks me back in here again.

I don't like trusting other people. That has never helped me before. I lick my lips, savoring the last of the broth that lingers there. Snuggling up to the fur blanket I have just pulled up to my chin, I let my eyes close. Before sleep steals me from this world again, I try to piece together a plan. My plans are never really good. But if the strong painkillers work for long enough, I may just have enough of a plan to eradicate more before Jeremiah tries to be a savior.

CHAPTER 28

Night time steals any natural light I previously had. My body aches, undeniable and constant.

I need to test my ability to move so I roll to my side, but the pain intensifies. "Fuck..." I grind out through my gritted teeth. Instantly, sweat starts to build along my lip line and a steady tremble hums through my body. I puff my cheeks out and force my legs off the edge of the bed. As soon as my feet touch the ground and I am in a sitting position, I give myself a few moments of reprieve by staying still like a statue. Jeremiah said nothing was broken but I am most certain every single one of my ribs is broken. If they aren't, I'd hate to feel the pain of broken ribs.

I stand, ever so slowly, tears burning at the edge of my eyes but I hold them back. I cannot cry. I won't let myself. I turn my head from side to side as I take in the pitch black surrounding and shuffle toward where I think I must have my candles. I have spent long enough in this place to have a mental map of the floor area.

I shuffle more, sure that my feet aren't even lifting off the surface at this point.

*Hmmm the bench must be here somewhere...*Lifting my hands when I know I must be near, my fingertips make contact with the rough edge. I flutter my fingers around and give a satisfied *hmm* when they land on wax tealight candles. Next, I move my free hand around as I try to find the hard flint. I smack over jars, bottles and nod to myself when I feel the cool hard surface of my stones.

I slide the candle closer to me so I won't lose it again, and grab a small piece of flint in each hand. I strike them together fast, spreading embers flying over the woodwork bench. It gives me enough light to find some twigs and shavings. I drag them close to me and heap them in a pile. I strike the stones together again, sending sparks scattering over the pile. I keep going, keeping a nice fast pace until smoke finally arises from the pile. The sparks keep flying onto the pile when I don't stop bashing the rocks together. More smoke arises. I blow down into the pile gently while adding more sparks. Finally, soft flames start licking at the cool air. The crackling of twigs and soft light warms my cold heart because the small task is the only thing that feels like it has gone right for me.

Quickly grabbing my candle, I angle it so the wick is inserted into a flame. The candle lights and I place it down before using the stones to stamp out the fire on my work bench. Walking around, I light a few more candles until I have enough light to see clearly.

I can't wait anymore. I push the pain away as much as I can and shuffle to my small window. The vibe is different tonight. I have looked out this window many times and judged everyone. I felt jealous of everyone, and some days my mood would make me glare at them all in envy. Now I look out and see a large unlit bonfire in the distance. There is a singular wooden pole in the middle. Meant for me.

I smooth my hair back away from my face and look around more. I can't see any women around. They wouldn't be though. I have only known of one human sacrifice and the women and children had to get themselves prepared perfectly in their black gowns, with their hair braided neatly and children all bathed so they were perfectly clean.

There are a few men trailing into the large meeting hall. They leave their homes and make their way up the man-made paths and shut the door behind them. Stupid secret bullshit.

I look back to the bonfire, with small fires surrounding it in metal fire pits. My eyes flick back to the meeting building and then back to the fires again. Fuck it.

I slowly move back to my bed and pull my black gown off the hook. It drags over the ground as I make my way back to the window. I grab the small hammer that I used to use to repair my cabin and start hitting around the outside of my window. The wooden frame is solid, old but solid in its place. I keep hitting the frame all around it, trying to loosen it.

"Shit..." I gasp and stop when a lone male walks nearby and makes his way to the meeting hall. Nervously, I look around, waiting momentarily to make sure he was the last one. When I am certain all the men are in there now, I give up trying to be neat and patient and smash the glass into pieces. Using the hammer, I break out the last of the shards around the frame and drape my gown over the bottom of the frame.

I start sweating more by just looking at the bench I need to lift myself onto. I need to. There's no other option. I look over my shoulder at the front door that is still locked. My eyes roam over the heavy hinges and rusty lock, assessing them quickly. Too old, too strong. There's no way I could barge my way through that.

I turn my head back to the broken window with the wind now free flowing in and making my long hair lash out, like it's angry at me. I blow out a breath and grit my teeth and lift my chin. The wind could also be cheering me on, telling me it is time for my big finale.

Using my hands, I lift myself up onto my work bench. Every single part of my body burns. The pain is so intense it doesn't just hurt, it feels like my body is burning from the inside out. Sweat accumulates on my upper lip and settles on the bridge of my nose.

I can't take in a deep breath to help steady my nerves. That will hurt my ribs too much, so instead I pant lightly. I wriggle closer to the open window, panting heavily. I clench my hands around the frame and pause to figure out how I am going to descend from this height. The window is so small that I can't turn around when I am halfway through.

Allowing myself a moment of humanity once more, I sob as I push myself through the window. Rolling onto the cold grass with a loud thud, I cry harder. "Come on body, you need to just make it through the next half an hour."

I swipe at my tears and clear my throat as I twist my long hair back and tuck it into my black cloak. While sitting on my knees, I look around, taking in the silence and stillness as a good sign.

Achingly, I move to a standing position and make my way toward the large communal hall. The closer I get, the louder the male voices become. Every time I hear a new deep voice, the fire within me burns hotter. The rage escalates and I'm only becoming more certain that my goal will be finished by the end of tonight.

My pace to the hall is slow, every time my toes dig into the wet grass, I tell myself it's a little closer to my destiny. The hem on my black gown drags with me, slowly, like a shadow engulfing me in its evil. The voices bounce between the multiple walls, conversing with each other like they aren't some of the sickest souls that ever walked this earth. I breathe the evil of my gown in through my nose and then breathe out, as if I'm releasing anything in me that isn't of the dark and evil nature.

A good person wouldn't do what I intend to do. I can't have any good inside me that could threaten to thwart my plans.

Creeping around the hall, I look for anything that can be used. My eyes settle on a rope and barbed wire that sit in a messy pile. Leftovers from the new addition to the laundry room.

I lift the rope and barbed wire in both hands and creep over to the hall. My foot touches down on the bottom step, a loud creek groaning as it does. *Fuck,* I scream silently to myself.

I am frozen in place. The only thing I can hear is my heart hammering in my ears. Can they hear it too?

Briefly, I wait a little longer and when I realize their talking hasn't paused, I make my way to the front door. I run my fingers lightly over the front of it.

I slip the rope through the two handles and wrap it round tightly. After I have secured a knot, I use the barbed wire for extra strength and thread it through before wrapping it around the handles. I ignore the pinpricks in my fingers and palm. It doesn't matter.

As soon as I am satisfied no one will be getting in or out now, I turn to the large bonfire in the distance. My eyes slide over the small fires surrounding it with a satisfied smirk tugging at my lips.

I creep over to them and stick two branches into them. After some crackling, I lift them in the air, watching the flames grow bigger on each branch. I turn back to the hall and make my way back over. I stick them under the open side of the small porch and push smaller twigs around both. I become mesmerized when the fire grows, my smirk turning into a full-blown grin.

Ignoring the growing pain in my battered body, I walk back to the fire pits and light more branches, bringing them around the back. Tall trees line the space with a small grass line between the building and them. Crows squawk loudly as I creep past the trees, holding my fire. I glance up to them with a smile and nod. Maybe they know. Maybe they are joyful too. Now being disrupted from their sleep, they rustle and move in the vegetation. I look at the small window that I know links to the cooking room. It's the only window in the large building. I crouch under it and put the two branches against the exterior wall. The wall isn't lighting fast enough so I dig my fingers into the lower pieces and tear at them. They move, bend but don't break. I keep pulling until a nail comes loose and it comes off just a little. I put one of the lit branches against it as much as possible and cackle when I see flames starting lick at the dry wood underneath. The flames grow. Centuries old wood, hard and dry. It's like gasoline to these flames.

Voices become louder.

"I can smell smoke."

"Did someone already light the bonfire?"

The voices grow louder, warier and more frantic.

I make my way back around the front and squeal in delight when I see the pillars on the porch alight. The color is beautiful.

I sit on the grass and rest my chin on my fists as I watch the flames engulf the building. The door thrashes. Bangs come from within when fists start beating at the walls. I hear glass explode and then screams follow soon after. I giggle to myself and let out a satisfied sigh.

Doors to cabins begin to open behind me. It's like an orchestra of thuds backing up the screams. Flames are everywhere now. It didn't take long at all.

I did that. I did all of that. Gasps and anguished cries are behind me but I keep smiling. They will all realize it's a good thing. It's the perfect ending. The only thing left to do is join them. I stand, taking my long gown off and dropping it to the ground. I step forward, fixated on the bright, hot flames. I close my eyes and smell the stench of burning flesh. The screams are painful now. They are burning alive. The only regret I have is that Jeremiah and Phoenix had to die with them. But I am sure they would have understood.

My eyes brim with tears, and my nose starts to sting when I try and sniff my tears away. There is a soft touch on my elbow and my attention follows the movement. *Skye*.

"Why?" she asks. Her eyes are big and round, looking at me like I have lost my mind. She is crazy. Doesn't she realize I have finally found it?

"Beautiful, isn't it," I answer her with tortured screams following my statement. "Skye?" I ask but look back to my artwork.

"Yeah?"

"Take them all. Get them all out. You can do what I never could. You can be the hero, while I stay the villain."

"Wha-what about you?" she cries at my back.

"I am ready. Go, take them all and never return," I assure her as I step forward again. I raise my arms on either side of me, holding them there as I move closer. The heat burns my face. I pause and smile widely. My entire body aches, but it does nothing more than remind me of what I have survived and what I have sacrificed. I really did it. I wasn't a hero to them, but I was a hero to myself.

There are no more screams. They are all dead. I scream loudly up into the night sky. Crows screech loudly and fly from the trees. They will move to a new home too.

I hear people running behind me. The children and women are leaving. Free.

I take another step forward, embers burning at my toes.

A few more steps, Violet, and peace will finally welcome you.

I lift my foot again and breathe out, ready to take a big leap into the flames.

"You couldn't just fucking wait?" a deep voice scorns me. The voice warms me. My body is slammed against a hard rock. I keep my eyes closed.

"If this is death, it's not so bad," I whisper.

"You're not dead, just fucking stupid," Jeremiah's rough voice growls against the side of my head. I open my eyes and blink a few times. A loud drumming heartbeat vibrates against my ear.

"I thought I had killed you," are the only words I can form in my shock. I was so ready for this to be the end of my horror story. I was never meant to get a happily ever after.

He scoffs and shuffles me away from the fire, still nestled in his chest though. "You wish I was dead, because when you are healed, I am going to punish you in ways you never thought were possible."

I finally push off him and look up into his face.

"Phoenix?" I wonder. My heart starts racing faster. If Jeremiah is alive, Phoenix needs to be. I can't live with one and not the other. I want both or neither. I take a step back, closer to the fire again. I can run and jump into it before he can stop me. He narrows his eyes on me and scowls.

"Don't you fucking dare," he warns me.

"Tell me."

An exasperated sigh leaves him before he steps to the side. Phoenix sits on the grass behind him. Dried crusted blood coats his nose, and purple hues coat every inch of his skin. But he manages to make me catch my breath when his intense gaze lands on me and he gives me a sadistic smirk.

"We were simply going to sneak you out. This is a bit dramatic, don't you think?" His smooth voice finds its way deep into my heart.

I step forward, away from the fire this time, moving closer to my Jeremiah and Phoenix. My knees shake, about to give way. Jeremiah catches me and helps me over to Phoenix. He lowers me to the grass beside Phoenix before he sits on the other side of me. All three of us face the fire and what remains of the cult. Jeremiah's arm wraps around me and pulls me closer to his shoulder. I lay my head against it and let myself truly be happy that they are all dead.

I was completely ready for my death, but now there is a glimmer of something other than a horror story for a life.

I don't know where we will go. Maybe we will stay here to live out the rest of our days. I don't know anything apart from the fact that I have my peace on either side of me. They were once the monsters in my story. They were once the ones I feared more than anything else.

Now they are the ones that have shown me trust can still exist. Someone can come to help me. Someone *will* come and save me. It just wasn't who I thought it would be.

TWO YEARS LATER

W ater rushes against my fingers, the coolness a soothing relief
from the later afternoon sun that beams over me. I smile to
myself when I see my reflection in the crystal clear water. This feels like
a dream. For two years, I kept thinking I would wake up and my body
would be getting dragged onto a burning fire. But every day I opened
my eyes in the morning was another day I would find a new piece of
myself. It's like a puzzle getting put back together, but being put back
differently. I was slowly pulled apart piece by piece, but the new me is
calm, happy and at ease with the things I did before.

I fill up our small bucket and turn to look over the meadow. We found
a new home. On accident. We walked and walked. For a long time,
the day after I burnt all the males alive, we didn't find civilization. We
walked further into the middle of nowhere. I don't think this land has
ever been touched by humans. Not in my lifetime anyway.

Across the flat meadow, and away from the rushing river behind me,
lies our cabin. Every month that passes we make improvements on

it. But the one-bedroom wooden structure is perfect in every way. It doesn't have any windows; it has one single door that Phoenix spent a week building. When we left the cult, the satchels I carried had medicines, herbs, dried food with some fur throws over my shoulders. Phoenix brought some tools, his small axe and more throws. Jeremiah brought some pots, fire starters and his hunting rifle with a box of bullets. It was all we needed. It's amazing how little you can survive off when the possibility of new life motivates you.

I look up to Phoenix, who sits on the porch in the distance while he scrapes debris from the rabbit skin Jeremiah pulled from his catch last night. Carrying the bucket, I walk across the meadow toward the cabin. As if Phoenix can feel my lingering gaze on him, his hands pause and he looks up to me. Our eyes lock and my cheeks flush. Two years later Jeremiah and Phoenix still send a heated feeling right through me, right to my toes. I reach the porch and step up onto it, giving him a soft smirk as I place the bucket down by the front door. He places the rabbit skin beside him, and in one sweep, he clutches my hand and pulls me down onto his lap. I straddle him and place my hands on either side of his face.

"I got the water for our rabbit broth," I murmur into his face. He smiles back and kisses down the length of my neck. Inviting him in, I tilt my head, arching my neck for him.

"I can see that." His words are muffled against the skin on my neck. Sweat trickles down my back from the unfiltered summer sun. Phoenix slides his fingers up my short tunic and glides them over my slick skin. I rock against his hardened cock and dig my nails into his bare shoulders.

"I like this dress on you," he says, showing me his appreciation for it by lifting it up and over my head in a frenzy. He tosses it to the side and drags his tongue over the hollow above my collarbone. I grip his shoulders again as I grind against his cock.

"And I like the lack of clothing on you during the summer. I never liked summer until now."

"I know what you mean."

He lifts me just slightly and takes his cock out of his pants. He growls when it's the entire way out, like he is talking to it, assuring it that it's about to get what it wants. What it needs. I settle down onto his cock with a long satisfied moan brushing through my lips.

My hands slide up and settle behind his neck as I move up and down. Our lips collide against each other in desperation. I want to touch every part of him. His tongue snakes out, exploring my mouth while his fingertips dig into my ass cheeks. I move faster, the pleasure building into that hot spark that spreads over my entire body, a thick layer of ecstasy covering every part of my skin. I whimper against his mouth when I am about to reach the peak. He grunts as his fingers dig in deeper.

A loud crash beside us makes me pull my mouth away from his. I hold still on Phoenix and look down at a dead deer that trickles blood over the porch. Its vacant open eyes stare up at me, or so it feels like.

"Oh by all means, don't stop on my account. Keep going while I hunt for all our meat," Jeremiah scolds us both. Phoenix shrugs and tries to move my hips again. I rake my gaze over Jeremiah slowly. Starting at his boots, then move up his strong legs, lingering on his hip bones and chiseled V line above his pants. I lick my lips as Phoenix moves me on his cock more as I explore Jeremiah's bloodied chest and shoulders before I reach his face. He arches an eyebrow at me like he is waiting for an answer. I lift a hand out to him and move over Phoenix on my own. Rocking deeply so I feel his cock against my cervix every time. Jeremiah's eyes burn with need and he steps closer to me, pulling out his cock. It's growing harder but not enough.

My hand grips around his cock. Clutching it tight, I slide my hand up and down, pumping it in the same rhythm my hips rock on Phoenix's cock. Phoenix groans into my chest, his hot breath colliding with my damp skin.

Jeremiah grows impatient and steps back.

"Get on your knees," he orders. We have all fucked together, endless times. Sometimes all day and all night, so I can't walk again the next day. We just work perfectly. All three of us are different, yet balancing. Phoenix lifts me off him, a deep frown settling over his face. He was close. I look down at his shiny cock that is coated in my desire and his pre-cum. We were both really fucking close. I crawl behind Phoenix and get on all fours, while Jeremiah moves behind me and Phoenix stands in front of me. He grips my hair and wraps it around his fist while he guides my mouth to his cock. Jeremiah slides his dick into me in one fast thrust. He slides it out again, so the tip rubs against the entrance. He rubs it up my pussy so it massages my clit a few times before thrusting it deep inside me again.

I grip the base of Phoenix's cock and slide my mouth over it, devouring it. Jeremiah thrusts in and out of me while his hand stretches under me and finds my clit. He rubs it up and down as his cock moves inside of me. We are all in tune with each other. Every single time. All three of us see each other's souls, hearts, demons and deepest desires. All three of us meet each other there every single time.

"Fuck…" Phoenix cusses as he slams his cock deep into my throat as he comes hard. I gag, tears streaming down my cheeks. Jeremiah presses hard on my clit and I shudder under his precision. An orgasm rips through my body as he buries his cock deep inside me, his cum filling me up.

Finally, Phoenix pulls his cock from me and crouches in front of me to swipe my tears away. "You may need a swim in the river now." He looks over my shoulder and rolls his eyes at Jeremiah. "You too. That blood is cooking on your skin in this heat," he finishes and stands straight.

"I'll pop the rabbit broth on like a good little bitch aye," he chuckles and walks around us toward the water beside the door. I stand, staying naked. I can now. We can do whatever the fuck we want. Cum coats my thighs, stealing Jeremiah's attention.

"We should bathe in the river. I don't feel like I am done yet. This hunter gatherer needs to collect on his payment," he says with a cocky smirk.

"I'm too sore," I counter and take three steps backward. He frowns and jumps off the porch to the grass in front of me.

"Violet…if you try to run and try to make a game out of this, my reward will be branding you again…" he growls, cracking his knuckles. I step back again and run a lone finger over the scars on my stomach. My mark that I love now more than anything.

"Violet..." he warns me again when I take two more steps back. He brushes his blood covered hand through his hair until it's well away from his face. It's grown out a lot more. Teamed with his short beard, sun-kissed tan and angry demeanor, he's begging to be fucked.

What can I say, we are still who we are. Jeremiah gets a bit *rough* sometimes and I pretend not to enjoy it, so he can get excited and be *rougher*.

The monsters in us come to the surface sometimes, and sometimes you have to say fuck it and embrace it.

With a loud squeal followed by laughter, I turn toward the river and start sprinting.

"Don't say I didn't fucking warn you, Violet."

The end

ABOUT THE AUTHOR

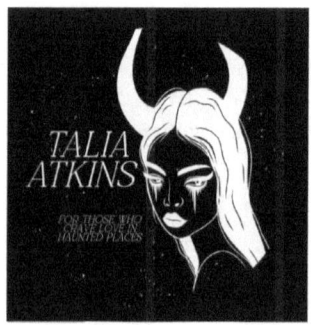

Talia Atkins is a proud Aotearoa author. Fairly new to the author world, she mainly writes dark romance and dark thrillers with a sprinkle of spice.

When not writing, she is a mum to five busy children, taxi driver to their many sporting events and working full time.

Want to follow Talia on her socials?
Check them out here.

ALSO BY

TALIA ATKINS

Trigger
Warnings

B ecause your mental health matters here is a list of possible tr!ggers that are throughout this book.

TW are but not limited to -

Pregnancy loss

Captivity

Live burials

Graphic Murder

Strong cult themes

Rape

Forced Orgasm

Self Mutilation/Harm

Suicide

Removal of body parts

Taxidermy of body parts

Incest

Stockholm Syndrome

Mass Murder